To See the Stars

by Jan Andrews

This seal though, it came alone and it came to us at Atterley.

TO SEE THE STARS

by Jan Andrews

with drawings
by Tara Bryan

For Jane Green, who welcomed Jan into her home in St. John's when she was researching this book. The two of them laughed and told stories of the heart together in the face of hard times.

"Shot silk," said the man the merchant sent to us in Atterley.

Star Struck

What it was got into me I'll never know. No, now, that's not true. I'll have to start different.

Truth is I can see it in my head still—that first sight of it— lying there beside all the other bolts of material. Like everything else was dead and it was alive.

"Shot silk," said the man the merchant sent to us in Atterley every year—end of the season when our catch of fish was all sold, when we had a bit of what passed for us as money. The man with the terrible limp that was set to selling because he couldn't do the ship work properly, I suppose.

"Shot silk."

The words were lovely in themselves. Right, too, for the colours. Red with dark, dark blue down under and inside somehow. Blue all bright and hidden. Blue I didn't hardly notice till that man put out his hand and picked up the loose end to move in the sun that had chosen just that moment to break out through the clouds.

Shot silk! I wanted to touch it. Had to. I wiped my hands on my skirt. I brought them up slowly. I was frightened almost because I could feel the little bits of skin catching, the little bits that stuck out all over from how I'd been working in the salt and the cod all summer long.

And that material! It was so soft and shiny. Once I'd reached out, I wanted to go on stroking it forever. It was so delicate, like I could have folded it till it was almost nothing. Not that that was what I wanted. I wanted to unroll the whole bolt there on the table. I wanted the red-blue sunlight spread out, covering everything else.

All the women were about, of course, clustering around the tables that had been put out down by the water, all in a line. The girls too—the ones that were a mite older than me— turning things over, admiring, comparing.

I couldn't hardly hear them. That material. I'd got mind for nothing else. I could feel my own skirt heavy all of a sudden. I wanted to tear it off me, all the thick rough gray of it. I didn't, of course. I couldn't be standing in my underwear, now could I, my petticoats hanging out?

Liz that was my special friend came up beside me. She saw what I was ogling. She giggled that giggle she had. The one when we were sharing stuff we weren't supposed to be talking about, like how our bodies were getting so strange on us. The one when we'd sit on her front step of a Saturday evening eyeing up the boys.

"How about for the dance then, Edie?" she whispered, before she moved on.

That material didn't mean to her what it meant to me. And there was the dance. The dance at Hole Bay to celebrate the end of the season. One week Saturday.

Words came to me. Words I didn't even hardly know I'd heard of. They had such a lovely ring to them: "Belle of the ball."

I looked round for Mum. She was considering whether she could afford a bowl with bright pink flowers on it. There was

one she'd a fancy for. I could see her touching the side of it—
just the way I'd touched my sheeny cloth. That gave me
some hope.

"Mum," I called out to her. "Come look."

She did too. She came where I asked her. She knew what
I was on about. I could see it from the way she shifted the
baby—Harry that wasn't walking yet—on her hip. From how
her mouth moved and her eyes were smiling.

She wiped her fingers on her skirt like I had. She reached
out with them just the way I'd done.

"Grand that'd look, missus," the merchant's man said to her.

The younger ones were crowding round by that time—
Will and Johnny and Winnie and Tess.

"It would too," Mum said.

"Can I have some?"

She looked me up and down, like no such thought could be
possible to her.

"For the dance," I went on.

"The dance?" she said to me.

"Next week at Hole Bay."

"You couldn't wear that."

"Why not?" I asked.

Another look came over her. A look that was angry almost.
She didn't answer. All of a sudden she was in a hurry, turning
away to where there was some rough brown woollen stuff,
fingering that.

"It's what I'm needing for your father's trousers," she
burst out.

She'd asked the price before I knew it. She was getting the
merchant's man to measure that woollen stuff out.

I couldn't let my silk go. Not just like that I couldn't.

I knew it had been a good year. I knew we'd caught plenty of fish. Hadn't I felt that in my legs and arms, my hands and feet and shoulders, as all of us had worked and worked?

"Just a skirt," I said.

"Winnie can have it after," I added, Winnie being the next one down.

"What is it with you?" Mum asked.

"Nothing's with me," I answered.

"It's only an old piece of material."

She set to, counting out the credit notes she'd got left over. The notes that were what we were given as pay for the fish the men had brought in in the dories; the fish that had caused me all that pain. The notes were to get our supplies in for the winter. They were little bits of paper with amounts written on them. The amounts stood instead of money. That's what I was talking about when I started out.

Mum acted like I was hardly there even. There was a red hot poker of hurting all up the middle of me. I didn't want to go on hanging about the way I would have done normally.

If I did, I'd have to see what Liz was getting, wouldn't I? Her mum gave her credit notes to have for herself. Her mum said she was old enough. Of course, in Liz's family, there weren't so many children. There was only her, but I wasn't going to let myself be considering that.

I went walking off along the shore, ducking under all the stages—the wharves—that were set there. After all, I thought to myself, it was like a holiday, wasn't it? I could go off if I wanted to. We weren't supposed to be working. The only reason the men weren't at the buying tables was that they were waiting till the women were done.

There were other things I thought too. About how I was like to die with being put upon: "Come on, it's your job, Edie." Sick to death of being the eldest girl.

That wasn't the worst of it. The worst was believing Mum thought I was too ugly. Remembering how she'd looked at me. How she hadn't even asked the price.

I'd got my head down mumbling to myself about it. I went past Greenwoods'—the last house in the community that stood all by itself though no one had ever been able to figure out why.

Greenwoods were strange. Not that I was really giving much mind to that.

I had my head set on a boy Liz and I had taken a fancy to at the dance last year. We'd found out his name was Roy. We'd talked and talked about his lovely thick black curly hair.

If I had the shot silk, surely he'd at least have to notice me. He might even ask me for a dance. Maybe more than one. He'd dance with me all night perhaps. Have eyes for no one else.

I kept on over the rocks till I didn't dare go any longer. Till I knew if I wasn't home soon—helping with the supper like I had to—Mum'd be worse than just plain mad.

As I went back, I got to picturing myself going to the dance in the dress I had already. A little-girl dress it seemed to me then. Blue, but not the blue that was in the shot silk. Blue that was washed out, faded.

When I passed Greenwoods' again I thought I heard someone calling. I did glance up but I reckoned I'd been tricked by the wind and the waves. I reckoned I'd been mistaken. The house was so quiet. Looked to me like no one was home.

And who would call? Not the mister or the missus. Him so stern and her so shy. Probably they were off berry picking. It'd be like them not to be doing what everyone else did.

Other times there might have been Jenny, the only daughter, the only child. She was a bit older than me but she might have called out. Wasn't she one of the lucky ones though? Hadn't she gone away? Wasn't she where she didn't have to ask someone else to buy whatever it was she wanted?

Mrs. Greenwood said she was in St. John's. She was working in some big house. There'd been a bit of talk about her going because no one had seen it, when usually there was some kind of a send-off.

Still, each time the mail came Mrs. Greenwood said she'd got a letter. She'd talk about that if she'd talk about nothing else. For a while, Liz and me had considered what Jenny might be doing. Not for long though. She'd not been like what you might have called a friend.

A couple of steps beyond Greenwoods' place and I was back into seeing myself going to the dance and looking like an idiot. Dad was home when I got there, with Jim and Pete my older brothers that went out on the water with him.

"You've got a face on you like you've sat on a wasp nest," Dad said, joking so the others all sniggered at me.

I stuck my tongue out at them when Dad couldn't see. I didn't forget my shot silk. How could I? When I'd organized the dishes and got Harry down to sleep. When I was in bed myself, upstairs where all of us kids slept in a whole long line so you could always hear someone breathing or snoring, I lay seeing it and seeing it. Red-blue brightness in my head.

It went on like that all week.

"Stop your mooning," Mum said to me.

She got angrier and angrier. Saturday she ironed the dance clothes for everyone. She had Winnie bring my dress. She handed it to me and set the flat iron back on the stove top.

"I've no more time," she told me.

"It doesn't matter," I answered.

"What do you mean?"

"I'll not be needing it."

"Of course you'll be needing it."

"Not if I'm not going," I flared out.

Dad happened to come in from where he'd been digging potatoes in the garden at that point.

"What's Edie on about?" he demanded.

Then it all came out.

"She says she's not going to the dance," Mum ranted. "We'll be gone all night. She can't be left here."

"She can't be spoiling things. I'll not have it. Not her, nor any of them," Dad replied.

He got into a bit of a to-do about all he'd had to manage by himself at my age. How he'd had his own boat because his dad got injured. He reminded Mum of how her life hadn't been so simple way back then.

All the others were there, their mouths open almost, waiting to see what was going to happen. Mum looked at them. I knew what she was thinking. She was thinking of all the long hours of all the summer. How even Johnny who was the littlest before Harry, even Johnny had been at it, bringing up the spruce boughs, shifting the salt fish that was drying on the flakes.

She looked at me pleading, but I wasn't budging. I wasn't going in that little-girl dress. I just would not.

"Your father's right. You suit yourself," she muttered.

There I was then when all the rest of them were setting out at last—Jim and Pete pulling on the oars for the dory, Dad with his fiddle, Mum with the food for the lunch. There I was settling myself on the rock beside the house. Pretending I didn't care. Pretending I was happy. Lifting my arm up to give them a wave.

Some sight it was. Everyone going. All the dories together and the oars all moving. Someone making the fiddle music already to give them a feel for what was to come. Not Dad. Dad wouldn't get his fiddle out on the water, I was sure of that.

The dories turned into specks and started disappearing.

"Good riddance to bad rubbish," I said to myself.

I had a bit of a pang when all the world seemed empty. When I realized from the whole of Atterley—apart from the gulls and the stirring on the water—there was not one sound. Still I couldn't afford to go on thinking about that. I figured the hell with it. If Mum thought it was all right to dress me up like a little kid I'd act like one. If I couldn't have my shot silk really, I'd do what I'd done when I was about the ages Winnie and Tess were. I'd pretend.

I knew it was daft but I didn't have to care about that at all, now did I? Not since everyone had gone away and left me. Not since, when I'd done my waving, mostly folks hadn't even been bothered turning round to look.

It was only Liz'd waved back. She was probably thinking her chance had come. Thinking she'd have Roy with his black curls flying all to herself there.

A skirt? A skirt wasn't enough. I needed a whole dress. Why not? If I was only dreaming I could have a dress, couldn't I? You should have seen it too, once I was through imagining. Sleeves that were tight so there was no dangling and flapping like with my ratty old sweater. A train behind me so I'd hear swishing. Breasts tight under so you couldn't help but notice. Breasts like the older girls had, only better. Breasts that could be seen.

Once I'd got it all planned I couldn't bear to waste it.
I thought I should do a tour of the harbour, the twenty houses
of it. I did too, walking with my back stiff and my head up high,
sending my arms out like I was giving things away. There was
this magazine had come to us. The new queen was in it.
Alexandra, her name was. If she could be Queen Alexandra,
I could be Queen Edie. No, I wouldn't be Edie. I'd be Edith—
my full name. Her Royal Majesty, Queen Edith. Sounded grand.

And who was to stop me? Didn't I own the place even
if only for that night? I went to the church. I stood on the
steps, all royal. I was tempted to do a bit of snooping in
people's homes. I could have easy enough. No one ever locked
their doors.

Hunger got the better of me in the end. My belly was
rumbling. There'd been so much cooking for the dance there'd
been no time for eating, apart from chunks of bread. Hungry
or not, I stuck with the queen show. Once I'd got home again,
I served myself regular old salt fish and brewis on dreamed-up
golden plates. A life with golden plates was getting to feel like
something I could be enjoying.

When the time came to light the lamps, I acted like I was
in a palace. I set a match to every one I could lay my hands on,
including the one Dad's granddad had got off a ship when he'd
gone swiling, hunting seals up the Labrador. The lamp with the
golden curlicues and tassels I wasn't supposed to touch.

I made myself good and comfy in Mum's rocking chair.
I was beginning to think how maybe I'd order up some
imaginary musicians. Fiddlers of my own to delight me. That's
when I heard the footsteps. They were coming along beside the
house. I stopped rocking and sat there frozen. I felt my heart
quit almost. All I could think was how it had to be a ghost.

After all I'd walked through all of Atterley without seeing hide nor hair of anyone. I'd watched every single person going out. Even old Granny Barnham that had to be carried wrapped up in blankets because she couldn't walk a step.

Every single one of my ideas of queenliness went from me. Sucked right out of me. Drained right down.

Next thing I knew the door was opening. For a moment I was certain: it was a ghost. It was really. Then I got to be more puzzled.

"Jenny? Jenny Greenwood?" I croaked out.

A great heap of questions came rising in me. I'd have asked them except I was too busy getting it into my brain, how I'd seen Mum like Jenny was, with Harry and with Johnny. With the others too, except then I was smaller. I'd seen most of the women in Atterley one time or another, their bellies fit to bust.

Jenny had tears running down her cheeks.

"I'm sorry," she said. "I am! I am really."

There was no doubt in me what she was sorry for. She was going to have a baby, looked like any minute. I couldn't get my feet to move. I couldn't go towards her. There was something lingering in me like she still might have the icy breath of death upon her.

Maybe a ghost would've been easier. My mind got into racing, mostly with fear and terror. Sure, I'd been around when Harry and Johnny were born. But I'd been hovering on the edges. And Jenny was bending over, clutching at herself. The contractions were coming.

I was fourteen. Fourteen wasn't old enough.

I listened to what was happening outside, hoping if I listened hard enough I'd hear someone making their way back over the water. Words came in my head I wanted to be calling.

"Oh, Mum! Mum, you've got to. You've got to come!"

But Mum wasn't going to come, now was she?

Didn't last long—Jenny and me standing there staring at one another in silence. Not more than a minute. The pains came on her stronger. She had to sit down. I found myself going forward, getting her in Mum and Dad's bedroom, that was right off the kitchen, telling her she should undress and get into the bed. That was what Mum would have done. It was. I knew it.

Jenny was so upset.

"I'll make a mess," she argued, but she couldn't argue much.

"Here," I said and I gave her Mum's nightie.

I told her I was going to make the fire up in the woodstove. I told her we'd need hot water. As soon as I was on my own again I knew what I wanted. I wanted to run. I wanted to show up at the dance in some left-behind dory like nothing had happened.

"Mum! Oh, Mum!"

I had to get on. An old sheet for the pulling. Go to the linen chest. Take the sheet out. Tie it to the end of the bed frame. Give it to Jenny. No mind that her belly under the quilt and the bedclothes was looking even more enormous. No mind she was sweating. Bring a cloth, all wet for cooling her forehead, like Mae Peet would have done.

Mae! She came, didn't she? She came always. For all the births.

I'd not been there with Mum alone. The only thing I'd ever needed to do was run Mae's errands when she'd said I was old enough. I couldn't think of that. I just couldn't. Nor of how now I'd have something to tell Liz she'd truly want to hear. I knew I shouldn't have let that idea even come into my head.

Jenny's hair was soaked. It was sticking all close to her.

I put the cloth on her forehead. I saw how her hands
were clenching on the bed sheets. I gave her the pull sheet
another time.

"Would you like a drink?" I asked her.

Mum wanted drinks always. Jenny shook her head.

There was kind of a lull. "I thought you were away,"
I said, because it seemed like I had to say something.

"Dad didn't want anyone to see me. He made me promise.
He kept me in the house. It was the only idea Mum could come
up with."

The pains broke in on her. She was hurting, hurting,
hurting.

"Mum—Mum was going to…"

Going to what? I wondered. I knew why her dad
had kept her apart, of course. A baby, and her not married.
It was the same reason Mum had told me when I first got
my monthlies: "You've got to be careful." A baby and not
married. That was a shame.

Jenny reached out and grabbed me. She held my hand
so tight it hurt. I thought how I'd heard her calling. It had
to be her, didn't it? I thought of her, shut in there, all that time.
I might have been only fourteen but I couldn't help myself.
I asked myself what everyone was going to be asking.
About the father. Who he was.

I wondered. I couldn't help that either. What it had felt
like when…. The thing—the thing inside her, making it.
The "thing" like my brothers had between their legs that was
something else to set Liz and me to giggling.

Jenny was on another track.

"Mum didn't want to go out tonight. Dad said she had to.
He said—at the dance…. It was what folks expected."

She was clutching my hand once more.

Wasn't what I believed, but I said it over and over. What Mum said when the little ones were fretting and sick with fever, "It's all right. It's all right."

Jenny got going again. "I was by myself. I got too frightened. I shouldn't have. I shouldn't have. I just–I just…. I saw the light."

That's how it went on, only there was less and less talking. More and more of Jenny just moaning, yelling, with me praying and praying there'd be some miracle. The dance would end early. Folks would start home before morning.

Some chance of that!

I wasn't being much use, except for another cloth and another. And for keeping the fire in. But I knew Mae always said a woman in labour needed company. I got a chair. I sat by the bed. I listened to the wind coming up, knowing it meant there was even less possibility of anyone coming home.

I tried not remembering. When Harry was born there'd been this time when even Mae had seemed worried. Jenny let out a scream. Her back arched. Her belly came up. Everything changed. It all got stronger. Her feet were pressing down and down into the mattress. She'd got the pull sheet all right. She was dragging on it so hard I thought the bed would break.

I wanted to run again. I knew we were getting to the difficult part. Even if in my head I could hear how Mae would be saying, "Won't be long now. Soon be done."

Mae who was so big and strong. Twice as big as Mum was. She'd go to the end of the bed. She'd lift the covers. She'd say over and over, "Come on, girl, you keep pushing. You just keep pushing. That's all you've got to do now. Push, now, push."

There were other things Mae did, weren't there? Things she'd been too taken up with helping Mum to let me in on.

"Time enough," she'd said after.

Time enough? I was going to have to try. Jenny had got her knees up, her legs were spread wide open. She was all stretched out and red there. There in that place where Mum had said I wasn't supposed to touch myself or look. But I had to look. Mae had said the baby needed catching.

I put my hands through the bed bars. I couldn't reach Jenny. There was only one thing for it. I climbed up on the mattress. I was kneeling in blood. It didn't seem to matter. The hot wet smell didn't either.

Jenny was pushing and pushing. She was screaming louder and louder. Louder and louder all the time. Then I was seeing something. It wasn't out far. It was only a little. I could have been mistaken. Except it seemed to be getting bigger. There was hair too. Black hair. Wet and plastered down.

Should I be pulling? I wondered. The round thing was the baby's head. I was certain. I felt my fingers cupping. Jenny gave a scream that made my ears ring like they'd be full of the sound forever. The baby's head burst out.

Now what? The rest of the baby seemed like it was stuck. I was going to pull. I was really. I wouldn't have just left it. Jenny gave one more heave. The baby came slithering. It came by itself.

It was so small and shriveled. There was stuff in its mouth. Mae had told me about that. She'd called me over. She'd shown me. How when there was stuff in the baby's mouth you had to get it out.

She'd had a cloth all ready. I hadn't thought of that. I took the edge of my sweater sleeve. I wiped the stuff away with that. There was a sound then. The sound was the baby crying. I was so happy I wanted to laugh. The baby was alive. It was alive and breathing. Kicking even. A girl. A little girl.

I'd have snatched her up into my arms. I'd have held her close up to me. I wouldn't have cared she was all sticky still. I wanted to feel her moving—the way I had with Harry. Mae had let me. She'd given him to me to carry. After Mum had held him, Mae had let me be the first.

The baby was still joined though, wasn't she? Joined by that cord thing that looked like a rope.

I had to cut the cord. I had to hurry. Mae had said that.

I propped the baby up. I don't know why.

I went to Mum's sewing basket. Mae had told me you could in an emergency. I reckoned this was an emergency. I found myself pausing over what color of thread I'd choose. I gave myself a talking to. Crazy! Crazy!

I got the scissors. They seemed so enormous. I didn't know how I was going to be able to bear to use them. Then it was over. I'd tied the cord with the thread in the two places like I was supposed to, holding my breath almost. I'd cut between the places where I'd tied.

The cord was cut but I wasn't snatching the baby up. I was taking her gently. I was wrapping her in the pull sheet.

"Look," I was saying to Jenny. "Here! Here, you can see her. You can see her. Look."

Even though there was more blood coming and a whole great pile of other stuff. Like fish guts, only thicker and heavier. I figured I'd come back to it later. I had it all planned out. How I was going to set the baby on Jenny's belly. That's what Mum had wanted. That's what she'd asked for right straight off.

Jenny turned away from me. She put her face to the wall.

"Look," I said again.

"I can't," she answered.

I thought she was too tired. I gave up thinking about the after-birth. That's what Mae had called it. I held the baby closer.

"Will I take her in the kitchen to wash her?" I asked.

I never did get any answer. Jenny was crying again. I started dithering, wondering how to help her. But the baby needed washing. It was what Mae did.

"I'll bring her back soon as she's ready," I promised.

I kept my promise too. I'd even got a diaper on her. I'd fixed her up fine for her mother. I'd found an old nightie from when Harry was so tiny. I'd got a blanket for keeping her warm. I'd done it all one handed—the baby in the other—the way Mum had shown me. I hadn't put her down except to dress her.

Jenny was facing the wall still. When she didn't answer me, I reckoned she was sleeping. I thought I'd not disturb her. I thought I'd just keep the baby with me, there in the kitchen for a while.

The baby seemed happy enough. She was good and quiet. I cuddled her up to me. I walked her round a bit. I talked to her, asking her questions: "What's she going to call you then? What d'you think of that lamp there? Isn't it pretty?"

She didn't understand, of course. That wasn't the point, was it? The point was to have her snuggled up easy, sleeping, making little baby noises, hearing a voice.

It seemed a long while. The house so quiet. Only the wind outside still.

I didn't know what to do with myself. I looked down at how my skirt and blouse were stained with all the blood and stuff. I thought maybe I should change them. I knew I should have put on an apron. Mum was always telling me.

It's odd but all of a sudden I was thinking too about my shot silk.

"You should've seen it," I said to the baby. "Ooh, it was lovely. Not as lovely as you though."

I gave her a kiss. Then I heard a movement. Surely now—surely—Jenny must be wanting a drink. I could change the sheets too. She must be uncomfortable in all that wetness.

The kettle was on the stove back warming like always. I moved it forward. I didn't want the baby to get cold. I put another blanket around her. I set her on the sofa. I settled her with a cushion against her. After all, I couldn't make tea one-handed. Even if Mum did. It was too much for me. I was afraid I'd spill something on the little one.

I got out the tea and the tea pot. I was reaching down a cup. I heard the bed springs. I reckoned Jenny must be feeling better. I turned to see her in the doorway, clutching the bedroom door post, propping herself up.

"You go back to bed," I said to her. "Mum always stays in bed for ages after. I'll bring you…."

"They'll come," she got out. "Your mum and dad."

"It's all right," I said. "You don't have to worry." I was pouring the tea.

"I can't be here," she insisted.

She hefted herself over to where she was leaning on the sofa end. The baby started snuffling. Jenny's hand went towards her, but it was like touching her child wasn't what she'd been intending.

"There's Dad. Everyone'll know. He never did want it—what Mum planned even."

I couldn't not be asking. "And what was that?"

"Saying the baby was a cousin's. Having me look like I'd come back home to bring it."

The baby snuffled louder. Still Jenny didn't touch her.

"I've nowhere to go. Nowhere to take her," she said. "Nowhere! Nowhere!" Her voice came stronger. "Nowhere. I should put her to the sea."

"You can't do that." I was across the room. I'd got the baby in my arms again.

"No," she said. "I can't."

Within a moment, she was out the back door. I don't know how she moved so fast but it was like the baby knew. She was howling, she was crying. She was thrashing against me.

"Don't you worry," I said. "We'll find her."

I've got to say it too. I did try.

I ran with the baby all over. I ran by the houses and the gardens. I ran by the sheds and the stages. I called and called. I ran until I couldn't run any longer. Until I had to stop to catch my breath. But it was night. I didn't know which way Jenny had gone even.

Anyway the baby had started into this whimpering. She wasn't crying any longer. She was making this sound like a puppy that Liz's dog had. A puppy that had died.

Seemed to me I should get her back home. I should go there, where the lights were streaming. I turned myself around but I'd come too far. The baby was getting weaker. Her weight seemed wrong somehow. I tried telling her her mum would come back. Her mum had to. Didn't make any difference.

"Jenny," I called out again. "Jenny."

That minute I was certain. Certain the baby was dying. Certain she was giving up. And there was the wind. It was pulling at my hair, my clothes. And we were alone in the nighttime.

Seemed like I'd tried everything. I can't say why I looked up. Maybe I was hoping God in His heaven would help me, that God that we all of us said our prayers to every night. However it may be, I tilted back my head.

I tilted back my head and I saw....

There'd been clouds before, when I'd been walking around, queening myself. There weren't any clouds any longer. Stars were filling the sky up. The sky was clear, clear, clear.

The night was so beautiful. Everything where I was—on earth—all wind and whirling, everything up above as still as it could be. That place that's called the Milky Way right over me. The Big Dipper pointing to the Pole Star—the star Dad used to steer by if he got caught late on the water—shining, shining bright.

Stars by the million all so gleaming. The blackness in between them, dark as dark.

A sight worth seeing. Worth it so I couldn't help myself. I held the baby up to look. A gust of wind came so strong it shook me. I felt her little body tighten like she was taking in this great gulp of air. She let out this big baby wail. There wasn't any more whimpering. That had stopped completely. She sounded like she'd sounded when she'd first been born.

I couldn't think of anything but her then, how I had to look after her. I had to get her inside. Seemed like the wind had given her an appetite. Seemed like she was hungry. I heated some milk on the stove for her. I gave her the milk to suck on with a cloth.

I kept hoping maybe Jenny would come back. I thought surely in the end the baby would bring her. Had she gone to the Greenwoods' place? I wondered.

If she hadn't....

I was afraid to go to sleep. For a long time anyway. Even though the baby was sleeping. I kept walking, backwards and forwards with her, pacing and pacing across the floor. I couldn't seem to talk to her any more. She didn't seem bothered.

My legs gave out on me in the end. I had to sit down. I chose the rocking chair because I thought I'd be more upright. Wasn't long before my head was nodding. I was afraid I'd let go. I was afraid she'd fall off my lap.

I got the two of us to the sofa. Just a couple of minutes, I thought. My head was so heavy. Maybe I slept long and maybe I didn't.

What happened next was it was light and I could hear voices. Next thing after Mum and Dad and Jim and Pete and Winnie and Will and Johnny with Tess carrying Harry were crowding in the room. They'd left for home early. They'd wanted to be sure I was all right. Mum looked shocked, but it was Winnie who came forward

"Is the baby yours?" she asked me.

Mum shushed at her. The words made me start crying. I don't know why. Once I'd got going, I couldn't seem to stop. The baby was wailing again. I reckon my crying had startled her.

"Jenny," I kept saying. "Jenny Greenwood."

Mum took the baby from me. She took her to hold.

"You've got to give it to us calm, girl," Dad said.

He pulled a chair out to sit on. Seeing him do that steadied me. Winnie held me round the shoulders to help me get through the sobbing. I didn't want to go back over it all, but I had to. The important parts anyway.

"That poor girl, there," Mum said, when I got to how Jenny had gone out the door and not come back.

"Only one thing to do." Already Dad was on his feet again.

He went out, nodding to Jim and Pete that they should go with him. Wasn't long before we heard the bell ringing like it did when there was a need for the men to go seeking someone lost on the water. There was calling to and fro and setting forth all through everywhere as soon as the other families came back from the dance.

Mum had me and the baby back on the sofa by that time. She'd found a blanket to cover the both of us. As she was tending to us, she kept looking at me and biting her lip.

"I got something to say," she blurted in the end. "That silk, I didn't want you to have it because I knew how grown it would make you look, and that frightened me. Still, it's good you were home tonight to do what was needed," she added.

"I'm sorry about the mess on the bed in your bedroom," I told her.

"No worrying for that," she said.

She didn't ask about what else I might have been up to even though I saw her looking at Great-Granddad's lamp that I'd got down. She just took the lamp and put it back on its shelf.

All day we waited. Mum kept the younger ones close. She wouldn't let even Winnie go far. Liz came to say the women were going searching on the land places—the women that could leave their children behind them safe. I wanted to go but Mum wouldn't let me. She said I'd had enough. She had the baby to care for, of course. She couldn't go either.

Mae stopped by. "There's not a boat of any kind that's missing," she told us.

"What are the Greenwoods doing?" Mum asked.

"The father's saying it couldn't have been Jenny. 'Wicked lies,' he's claiming. The mother's gone invisible," Mae replied.

I thought about what Jenny had said about the baby and where she should be put to, but I kept that thinking to myself. They found her body along the coast a couple of days later. It was lapping against the rocks. Maybe she'd slipped and fallen, weak as she must have been, folks said about it.

No one wanted to be talking about any other kind of "maybe." It'd have meant we couldn't have a funeral for her in our little church. Mum and Dad had to make the arrangements for that because the Greenwoods had left already.

"Done a bunk in the nighttime," was what Mae said.

The funeral felt awful. The minister came from Hole Bay for it, like he always did for such things. We didn't have a minister ourselves. There weren't enough of us in Atterley so we couldn't go to church as often as we might.

All through when he was talking I was looking at his white, white surplice and thinking there was more I should've done. I broke down during the hymn. I started crying again. Mum had to give the baby to Winnie and bring me out to comfort me. We were calling the baby Janie by that time. We'd taken her with us because, like Mum said, we had to. She was Jenny's only kin.

The service was one thing. Having the coffin put in the ground was another. I didn't want to be hearing those words, "Ashes to ashes, dust to dust," but that was what was always said.

"It's not nothing that you saved one of them, you know," Mum said to me after it was all over.

I was thankful for that, I was really. I almost told her how I'd held Janie up to see the stars but I didn't. I'm not sure why. I didn't tell anyone. Not even Liz. I was afraid a bit people would think I'd done something stupid. More it was like a secret—a mystery I wanted to be having for myself.

We kept little Janie. Of course, we did. She was another mouth to feed but there wasn't any question as to her going any place besides our house. I never did get my sheeny silk, although I still would've liked to. I still thought it was the loveliest material in all the world.

That—what I said—about a mystery. The feel of it came back to me. It came back more than once. I'd watch Janie doing the things babies do, sucking her toes and rolling over and the like. Inside me I'd have the thrill of it. The moment when she took that wind-breath, the moment she decided to be living. I didn't understand why it meant so much to me. But, oh, it did. It did.

*"Now, Edie," Mr. Alexander Brodie said, "This is the household
I have selected as perfect for you."*

Seal of the Harbours

The summer after Janie was born, when I was fifteen years old and getting to put my hair up of a Sunday—that was the summer the seal came. It wasn't the kind of seal our granddad had been after when he'd gone to the ice, Dad said. It was the kind folks saw, there by the beach at Hole Bay in the springtime sometimes. Usually there'd be several of them.

This seal though, it came alone and it came to us at Atterley, where we didn't see seals ever except for a distant head out bobbing on the water. This seal came and then it stayed. A female, Dad said. He said you could tell by how she was smallish. He said there was something in her face too, although he didn't go on to say what that might be.

"Good flipper pie, she'd make," he'd add in the beginning.

Still he didn't do anything about going after her. Strangely, there wasn't a man could take a gun to her nor a boy could throw a stone, even if we did have reason enough that year to grab whatever came by.

Her skin now—it was grey with rings of dark set on it. Pretty to see. She'd be on the rocks and she'd be in the water.

She'd come up under the holes in the stages where the fish guts went down when the men were doing the cutting after they'd brought the catch in, when there was catch that is.

I started looking out for her. I'd go of an evening to perch myself near where I knew she'd be lying most likely when she came ashore. At the place under the cliff where the rocks were flattest. She'd be on her side, her eyes so big, her flippers hanging down.

I'd sit there quiet with her, off at some distance, so she wouldn't be frightened. I tried taking little Janie to look. I took Janie wherever I could, I loved her so much. Still, there on the rocks it wasn't really safe for a baby. And Janie was too much of a wriggler, wanting to get on with her crawling and pulling herself up to stand.

"'Eal," she'd call out, too, in her baby talk, and the seal would get disturbed.

Other summers I wouldn't have hardly had the time, but the catches were so dreadful there wasn't that much work. We had more space for doing nothing than I could ever remember. That's how it was Liz and me had got our rear ends perched on our front step in the sunshine one Friday afternoon in August, having a good old chat.

We were going at it nineteen to the dozen when all of a sudden Liz paused.

"Well now, Edie, isn't he the fine one!" she said to me, digging me in the ribs.

A fine one indeed, I thought to myself. Walking along so jaunty, like there was a laugh to him. A man, too. Not one of the boys we were mostly there to be watching out for. Wearing a suit such as we'd not seen on anyone in Atterley— or anywhere else we'd been—ever. A suit that was lighter

and not so stiff. He had this nice little round hat on his
head too.

We didn't *decide* to get to our feet exactly, I don't think.
We certainly didn't say anything about it to each other. It's just
that before we knew it we were walking after him. Following
him. Trying to keep a respectable distance and not making
much of a job of it. Catching up to him without even meaning
to. Or so we pretended to ourselves.

Lo and behold, he stopped and turned toward us. He took
off his nice little hat and gave us a bow.

"Mr. Alexander Brodie at your service," he said and, oh,
his voice had such a lovely smoothness to it.

"Can we help you?" Liz asked.

Turned out he was some sort of a long lost cousin of Liz's
mother, or so he claimed.

"Keeping up family ties," he told us, for why he'd come
visiting.

What reason had we to doubt that? Fact is we had none.

When he said he could find jobs for Liz and me in the city,
casually, like he'd only just thought of it while we were sitting
in Liz's kitchen later, with Liz's mother giving him a cup of tea.
When he said that, we couldn't help but be all of a flutter.

I said already, didn't I, how girls would go from there—
to St. John's—like Jenny Greenwood was supposed to have
done. And, oh, when they came back… I mean, Mae Peet's
Sarah had only just set off again after a week with us.

She'd told us about the wonders. Things we'd heard of
before but could never quite get enough of hearing about again.
What it was like to turn some little gadget called a "tap" and
have water come out of it so you didn't have to be going to the
well all the time. How there was this *ee-lec-tri-city* for the lights

so you wouldn't need to be messing with lamp oil. Liz and me had sat with our eyes wide listening to her. We'd asked her what she had to do. She'd said it was "only old housework." She'd said it wasn't harder than what she had to do at home, excepting that there she was paid for it. She'd made it sound easy.

Liz now—Liz with her golden curls. She'd got what Mum claimed were itchy feet on her. I felt like maybe I ought to have them too. I felt like it was our turn. I didn't hold back then when it came to saying how maybe it would be exciting. Maybe it was a thing that we should do.

And there was Mr. Alexander Brodie. Who wouldn't want to be going with him? He wasn't just any old body either, was he? He was Liz's relative. That meant a lot to her mother and father even if neither had heard tell of him before.

With Mum and Dad it was harder. They had to be asking him a whole lot of questions, one evening when he'd come over after supper for just such a purpose. They wanted to make sure I'd be properly looked after.

I could see though the more he talked about my wages, the more they were thinking about how they were going to be needing something extra to get them through the winter. How good it would be to have me sending actual money back, seeing as how there'd be almost nothing coming in through the way of the credit notes.

In the end it was what I'd done with little Janie settled it.

"You delivered a baby, I suppose you're old enough if that's what you're wanting," Dad said.

"It is what I'm wanting," I got out.

Everything happened so fast after that. Mr. Alexander Brodie had to be off, he said. Before I knew it—the next day almost—Mum was helping me get my things together to put in the little carpet bag she'd found me. My Sunday clothes, with the long black skirt. My aprons she was certain I'd be needing. She was having a bit of a cry over the packing.

I was trying not to. I was trying to look like there was nothing in me except eagerness to be gone. That was how Liz was. I was certain. I was eager too. I really was.

The last evening we had a special supper, all of us at the table, all ten of us. I thought Dad might kill a chicken but he didn't. The chickens were too precious. Food for later. I knew that.

I put the little ones to bed like I always did. I gave my Janie an extra hug. I took myself out for a walk. I didn't want to admit it to myself even but I was drinking it all in. How the stage heads jutted so far into the water. How the houses were set, dotted all about. The church high up by Liz's house, next to the school the families had managed to get together to pay the teacher for when mostly there was nothing to spare for anything. The brook with its tea-brown water. The brook I'd crossed so often on the stepping stones that had been set down ages back.

I was almost to the place where the seal would be when I heard footsteps behind me. It was Dad.

"You'll not be minding if I go with you where you're going, will you?" he asked me.

I gave a bit of a shrug but actually I was glad to see him. Surprised, too.

"I know you've been watching her," he said when we got there, when we were both sitting looking at her now.

"Do you think it could really happen?" I asked him after a while.

"What would that be?" he answered.

"Like in that story you tell us—the story you had from your dad. You know, about how the seals can come out of the sea and take off their skins and play on the land."

"The one I don't tell outside the family because there's no one else in all the world would believe it, and I don't want everyone in Atterley thinking I've gone off my head?" Dad was shifting his pipe around.

"The one that's *ours*. That Grandad told you he got from some come-from-away fellow that had fetched up here from Scotland."

It was there then, between us. How when Dad gave out that story it was like he had to. Once a year usually. Darkest winter. All of us in the kitchen by the stove. How he'd always make us promise we'd not be telling it to anyone else. How that made it special to us.

How the seals on the land were happy. They were dancing. A man came. They didn't see him. He found their skins in a pile. He took one for a blanket to warm himself with. Turned out it belonged to a seal maid. She went after him. She asked him for it back. He looked at her and he loved her. He made her go with him. He hid her skin so she couldn't find it, so she had to be his wife.

I was hoping Dad might just tell it there on the rock but I knew that was expecting a bit much. "Must have been some hard," I said finally. "Not being able to get into the sea again. Not being able to be free."

With that our seal lolloped off. She slid into the water. Dad took my hand to hold like he hadn't done since I was small. He took my hand and we went home.

Everyone came to see us off next morning—everyone. There was a lot of waving and calling out to us. Mum was crying again and Liz's mum as well.

"You do us proud," Dad said. "You see to it."

He kissed me on the cheek. Jim and Pete now, they looked like maybe they'd a hankering to be going with me. Winnie and Will and Tess kept saying how much they'd miss me. Johnny and Harry were a bit confused. I took Janie up but she squirmed away because I was holding her too tightly.

I'll not bore you with the details of all our travels by sundry carts, along cliff tops and through small forests to get to some place Mr. Alexander Brodie didn't even bother telling us the name of.

"A mere way station," was what he claimed.

I expect we should have been disturbed, Liz and me, when he added two more girls to the party. Twins. Bessie and Mary, their hair all long and dangling. Not saying "boo" to anyone. Dressed still in pinafores, not like us.

We should've been disturbed maybe, but we were too busy looking the pair of them over, deciding they weren't going to be much in the way of competition. Letting Mr. Alexander Brodie hand us down like we were ladies—like I was queen for a day or something. Listening to his talk about how there were streetcars in St. John's that went with nothing pulling them, no horses. Making it sound like where we were going was into palaces near enough.

We had to get to this "way station" place because that's where the steamer went from. It was waiting when we got to the dock. No time for looking around then. We were going up the gangplank. We were setting off.

It was just like from the start. I didn't know whether to be pleased or sorry, even with Liz nattering away beside me, pointing out this, that, and the other thing, clinging to my arm. We all stood together as the steamer pulled out. Seemed like

what you did. After all, there were folks there waving,
even if we didn't know any of them.

So big a boat it seemed to me, with all the people on it.
Once we'd got launched, the others went below. I didn't.
I didn't want to. I wanted to be out in the open. Even though
it was mauzy. Even though I might get myself a bit wet.
I'd never been on the water hardly, except for little trips like
going to the dances. The water was the men's place. I wanted
to watch how the waves stretched. I wanted the wind and
the smell of it. Anyway, Jim and Pete had told me the best hope
for stopping myself getting seasick was staying up top.

I chose a seat then by the railing. I pulled the shawl Mum
had given me to put over my coat about my shoulders. It was
special, that shawl. Mum's mum had knit it for her when she
got married. I knew what it meant to Mum, parting with
it for me.

I think Liz thought I was crazy but I didn't care. I watched
the buildings disappearing. I saw the lighthouse. No seals,
I thought to myself. No seals there on those rocks.

Liz came up now and then. She said I should go down.
I wouldn't. I was determined. I could see, anyway, each time
she came up she was looking less healthy.

As for the others… Liz informed me Mr. Brodie was
playing cards with some men he'd met. She said Mary and
Bessie were sort of huddling. She said they needed looking
after.

"The silent wonders, they are."

A day and a night and then some the journey took.
The smoke coming out of the smoke stack into the sky to be
carried on the air. The engines rumbling. The gulls coming
sometimes and sometimes going away.

We stopped at one place and another. People got off and more got on. The steamer was fuller. We started up again. I made myself a nest almost. All my things around me. I nibbled on the bread and lassie sandwiches Mum had made me. Mostly there wasn't any shore to be seeing. Mostly there was just that water, like I said.

At last though, land was appearing in the distance. Land was coming near. A man that was close by me said it was Cape St. Francis. I tried to remember where on the teacher's map in the school room Cape St. Francis might be.

A lot of folks were coming up the stairs from below and onto the deck by that time. It wasn't hard then to reckon something was about to occur. More and more on the voyage I'd been feeling easy. I'd been enjoying myself almost.

Liz had made a few more visits. She'd told me about this other fellow she'd got her eye on as well as Mr. Alexander Brodie. I'd had a few daydreams about the money I'd be earning. What I'd be doing with it.

As we got nearer to the land I came to be more worried. While we were chugging our way along where we could see the rocks and the waves breaking and the houses in the coves, I found I was clutching the railing so tight my hand was aching with the strain.

Mr. Alexander Brodie came up on deck like everyone else did. He brought Bessie and Mary with him. They looked at me as if they'd forgotten who I was. I thought how it would be like to not be able to be told apart from someone. Even your sister. Liz was all a-twitter.

"You wait," Mr. Alexander Brodie said to us. "There's a sight soon for you to be filling your eyes with."

There was too. We went in through this narrows—the cliffs so towering high above us on either side. The steamer's horn got into hooting and tooting. There we were then, with everyone crowding along the railings again. In the harbour—the harbour of St. John's.

Wharf upon wharf upon wharf, great big structures I'd never seen the like of. I couldn't get over it. How every place I looked seemed to me to be plimmed to the gills with people. Boys pushing hand carts, all loaded down with wares. Men, shouting and giving orders, checking things off on lists that were clipped to boards they were holding. Folks all over. More than I'd ever imagined.

I didn't know whether to be excited or terrified. I was afraid the terrified was winning. I was afraid Liz would feel it as she leaned with me over the rail.

"Isn't it something then!" she said to me. "Wouldn't they be amazed back home now, seeing us!"

"Yes, yes, they would," I answered. At least I could be truthful about that.

Next thing that happened was there were cables being thrown out so the steamer could be tied up to the shore. We were caught in this surging and pushing. Everyone was hurrying. I'll never be sure how I got back down the gang plank and onto dry land. There I was though, standing and gaping all around me. Taking it in how back from the wharves there were stores. Merchants' premises and such. Even more people.

There were ways it wasn't so strange, of course. The good old smell of fish, for instance. The need to be watching where I was putting my feet because of the fish muck. But it was all so much bigger, like I was being crowded to nothing. I lost touch with the others. That frightened me. Even Bessie and Mary were a welcome sight. Even better was seeing Liz and Mr. Alexander Brodie once again.

He was off in an instant. I knew I should be paying more attention to where we were going but I couldn't seem to do it. There was too much noise. It was coming from every direction. That streetcar thing he'd said about. It was right in front of us swaying and ringing its bell and clanging. Horses too. Horses everywhere. Clipping and clopping and pulling these great enormous rumbling contraptions behind them.

Best I could do was keep my eyes on the back of Mr. Alexander Brodie's little round hat. There were cobblestones under my feet. At least I supposed that's what they were, seeing as how I'd only ever heard about such things.

Before long I realised the cobblestones had run out. The roads were dirt like the one in Atterley, like we'd travelled on to get to the steamer. We were leaning forward more, and puffing. The ground was getting steeper. We were going up a hill.

"Best foot forward," Mr. Alexander Brodie said to us.

It dawned on me things had got a bit quieter. I wished we could go slower. I wanted to look properly. I was about to say something about not so much hurrying to Mr. Alexander Brodie but he stopped. The rest of us stopped as well.

I took it in how what we'd been walking on were streets. We didn't have streets in Atterley. We had roads and lanes, but not streets.

"Is this one house then?" Liz asked, pointing at the great place in front of us.

"Oh, no," Mr. Alexander Brodie replied.

That made me take another look. I saw there were four big doors with four sets of steps to get to them. I'd never thought

of houses joined in a row before. It came to me maybe
we were all going to be working right next door to each other.
Liz and me at least. Liz and me for certain.

"Now, Edie," Mr. Alexander Brodie said. "This is the
household I have selected as perfect for you."

So much for that. I was to be on my own, was I?
Comfort was, the house looked grand. Tall so it went three
big floors upwards. Tall with great wide windows to the front
of it, bulging out with a grace to them, lace curtains hanging
down inside.

All at once I was proud. Seemed like an honour, being
the first one chosen, especially as Liz was looking disappointed.
Especially as Mr. Alexander Brodie was holding out his arm.
Being proud helped me draw myself up a bit. More Queen
Edith!

After all, I'd never walked on a man's arm before, even
if it was an alleyway we were going down, even if we weren't
going up those big front steps. The others came following
behind us. It was quite the procession.

When we got to the back door Mr. Alexander Brodie
knocked.

"See what I've brought you, Cook," he burst out when
it was opened. "This here—it's Edie. Edie Murphy. Didn't
I promise you?"

I tried not to notice how Cook didn't look all that pleased
to see me. I tried to concentrate on how she had this little
white starched cap thing on her head, how she was wearing this
white starched apron. How her hair was greying at the edges,
drawn back in this bun. How—apart from the apron and the
cap, of course—she was all in black.

"You're to come in," she said.

"You others should wait outside," Mr. Alexander Brodie ordered.

In I went then, down these stairs. Down? That seemed odd to me. Odder still to find I was in a kitchen that was underground. It had to be a kitchen though. Seeing there were pots and pans hung all over. There was a long scrubbed table. There was a stove that was taking up the half of all one wall.

"I'll tell the mistress," Cook said.

Nothing else? At home, a cup of tea was always offered. Apparently tea wasn't what Mr. Alexander Brodie expected. As Cook went off, he nodded. He stepped over to the table. He pulled out a chair to sit down on. He left me standing there, clutching my bag and waiting.

I glanced up. I saw Liz peering through the window, waving to me, poking her tongue out. I didn't do anything. I didn't wave back. It was all so strange. The room even. Big as three kitchens, bigger than any I'd ever set eyes on.

"Mrs. Toms will see you," Cook said, when she got back again.

"Mrs. Toms will be your mistress," Mr. Alexander Brodie told me. "Cook will take you to her."

Mistress? I didn't like the way he said it. I went with Cook anyway. What else was I to do? I'd Mum and Dad to be thinking of. Dad telling me to make them proud.

Up we went and along a hallway with a great wide staircase curving into it. Cook opened another door. We were in a room that was filled with all sorts of finery. Deep, deep carpets, furniture that was gleaming it was polished so much. Not that I could really be looking. All I could be seeing really was this old woman, holding herself so straight backed, sitting in a chair. She had eyes that went right through me. Didn't take much to guess she was the mistress. She was Mrs. Toms.

"This is the girl, madam," Cook said, giving a little sort of a curtsey.

I hung back. "Stand before me," Mrs. Toms ordered.

Everything in me turned to water, but I did it.

"You are to hold out your hands," she instructed.

I held my hands out the way she said.

She looked at them like she expected they'd be dirty. She looked at the rest of me like I was probably dirty all over in fact.

"These are the hands of a working girl," she said to Cook at last. "A working girl is what we are needing. She is from a good family?"

"Yes, Madam."

"She knows there will be training?"

"I'll make certain, Madam."

"We shall start with tea. She will bring it in half an hour and she will be wearing a uniform."

Her voice was sharp. It was cutting.

"I shall see to it."

Another little curtsey. Back we went to the kitchen. Mr. Alexander Brodie was getting to his feet.

"The usual arrangement," he said. "To be taken out of her wages."

Cook sniffed. She sighed a small kind of a sigh. "The usual arrangement," she answered.

That's when I realized he was getting money for me. Cook was giving it to him. She was fetching it from a drawer in this dresser where there were plates stacked. He was counting it, like Dad counted the credit notes when he sold the fish.

"Good luck to you," Mr. Alexander Brodie said to me as he was leaving.

It's more than luck I'll be needing, I thought.

Liz was waving again. I still didn't wave back to her.
I was too busy, knowing I was in for a whole lot more than I'd
bargained for.

"Uniform first," Cook said.

Why hadn't it entered my head I wasn't going to be wearing
my own clothes? I reached for my bag. At least I had my aprons.
Cook took one glimpse at the brown, rough brin of them.

"Well, they'll never do," she said.

Isn't there even a hello here? Don't I get even a moment
to get to know you? I wondered. The answers were pretty
obvious.

The uniform didn't fit. It had been made for the last girl
who was smaller. I couldn't move properly in it. It was this
stiff kind of fabric, tight across the shoulders. Apparently that
didn't matter. It didn't matter either I thought black was for
funerals—like we'd had for Jenny. It didn't matter I didn't want
to be putting my hair into this net thing so I could be wearing
my own little starched white cap.

There I was half an hour later, to the dot exactly. Lifting
this tray Cook had set up ready. Loaded with the silver teapot
and the cup and saucer of thin, thin china with painted flowers
on it. The small plate with the cookies and the bowl with the
silver tongs for lumps of sugar. The milk jug. The jug with hot
water. Going up the stairs again. Trying to get the door to the
parlour open without spilling anything. Trying not to trip.

I'd poured tea before, of course I had. I'd been pouring
it for Mum as long as I could remember. This though—this was
nothing like that. I had to set the tray down on a little round
table. I had to step back for Mrs. Toms' inspection. I had to get
the tea into the cup with just the right amount of milk and her

not saying a word to me to tell me what "right" might be.
I had to listen to these little coughs she made to show me
whatever it was I was doing I should be doing it different.

Her all the while sitting there peering at me whenever
she felt like it through her spectacles on a stick. Her face white
powdered, her hair swept up from her wobbly old neck in this
elegant swoop of a thing held tight with combs. The room
so silent each time I moved anything it seemed like I was
making a clatter. I was disturbing the peace.

"I believe you have much to learn," was all she said
to me when she was finished. There was never a "please"
or a "thank you."

I was a wreck by the time I got back to the kitchen.
I'd not been there two minutes. I'd hardly started washing
the tea things like Cook told me I had to. This bell rang.
It was high up on the wall. In a whole long line of bells with
words written under them.

"See what it says there. It says *Parlour*. Parlour's your job.
She's wanting you," Cook said.

"I will have a glass of water," Mrs. Toms told me.

That was it. I was at her beck and call. I brought the water
on a smaller silver tray. There was nothing to be put into her
hands directly. Cook informed me about that.

"You may go," Mrs. Toms told me when she'd got what
she wanted.

You may go? I had to have her permission just to step
outside the room? I took myself back to the kitchen. I finished
the tea dishwashing, praying and praying that bell-thing
wouldn't ring again. Cook said I shouldn't be wool-gathering.
There wasn't a minute to waste. She said I should be looking
around so I'd know where things were when I had to find them.

The ladles, for instance—the ladles that were on the hooks by the stove there. The cutlery that was in another one of the dresser drawers.

I haven't said, have I? Even doing the dishes. It wasn't so easy. It was like Sarah had told us. There was this tap gadget. I kept turning it the wrong way. I kept having the water spurting all over me. I wasn't quick enough, shutting it off. I got more water in the sink than I needed.

Me that was the eldest girl, that could pretty much have run our household if I'd had to? Me, the eldest girl, not doing anything right? There were switches for the lights. I didn't know how to find them. When I did find them, I didn't know how they worked. It didn't occur to me I was supposed to take the white apron off in the kitchen and put on another one and then put the white apron on again when I went upstairs. I got the white apron dirty. Cook had to find me another. By then she was into getting supper.

She set me to slicing potatoes. I didn't do them fine enough. That meant they had to be done over. I could feel my face getting hotter and redder. Supper when we finally got to it was to be in the dining room. More shiny wood—a great long table of it that I had to lay. At least Cook took me up there ahead of time to show me how to do it.

A knife and a fork for fish, a soupspoon, a little knife to butter bread with, a bowl for soup, a plate for "the main course" and a knife and a fork for that as well, a side plate, another water glass with another glass beside it, a fork for eating what Cook said was "dessert." More at the one seat than we had in our whole house it seemed almost. Everything in some sort of special order. Even if Mrs. Toms was a widow. Even if she'd be eating by herself.

"It'll be for you to serve," Cook said.

"How will I know what to do?" I asked her.

"Let's just say you won't have much trouble knowing when you're wrong," she answered.

That was it though, wasn't it? Wrong was all I could be.

How could it be different? There wasn't anything at home about putting plates down from the right and taking them from the left, now was there? There wasn't anyone serving anyone. Not like this. Mum dished the food out but she didn't arrange it any particular way. It was all recognizable to me. There weren't any little curlicues of anything.

Most of all, there wasn't Mrs. Toms and her coughs. I had to stand behind her again. Like I'd done at tea time. I could see her body begin in on this stiff sort of tremble. I'd know another complaint was coming.

Supper wasn't even the end of it. After supper, I had to go upstairs to Mrs. Toms' bedroom. I had to turn down the sheets. I had to pull the drapes closed. I had to wait till she was almost ready to go up. I had to bring hot water to put in a jug for her to wash herself. I had to put her clothes away and help her into bed.

Somewhere in there I think Cook and me had our bit of supper but I can't remember it. I can't even remember feeling hungry, though it was hours since I'd eaten. On the steamer, most like.

The thing I do remember is Cook making me this list in tiny writing I couldn't very well read. It was a list of the things I had to be doing in the morning before anyone else was up. Light the stove and get it warming. Put water into the stove container to be heating.

Go out and sweep the front steps. Scrub them and make sure there wasn't any speck of anything left on them. Scrub

the table in the kitchen so Cook would have a good work space.
Clean Mrs. Toms' shoes that I'd brought down with me when
I'd finished in her bedroom. Polish them till they were shining.
Give my own boots a going over while I was at it.

The list was one thing. The instructions that went with it—
that Cook just talked to me about—were another. Seemed like
there wasn't a single thing that didn't have to be done some
special way. I had to be careful too because Mrs. Toms would be
checking. Most important of all was how I wasn't to be making
any noise. I wasn't to be waking Mrs. Toms before she was good
and ready.

I did get to go to bed at last but it was up in this little room
at the top of the house. I'd never been so high, not for sleeping.
I was afraid to look out of the window. Harder was the fact I'd
never been in a bedroom without the sounds of all my brothers
and sisters all about me. I wasn't used to such emptiness.
There was Cook's list to be thinking of too. I couldn't get
myself settled.

I suppose I dropped off finally but it seemed I'd hardly
got my eyes closed when it was time to get them open again.
I took Cook's list but everything was all so complicated. Just
finding my way about the house for one thing. Three great
bedrooms, besides the one Mrs. Toms had with a little dressing
room beside it; the downstairs rooms. There were so many
doors. I got lost trying to find the kitchen.

That took time up—time I didn't have. I managed to get
everything done but it was only sort of. I knew I'd been rushing
too much. I couldn't go back and do any of it over though,
could I? Cook was putting Mrs. Toms' breakfast on a tray for
me to take up to her. Her in her bed still with the shiny
comforter that was on it. Not a handmade quilt—the only bed
covering I'd ever seen before—in sight.

After she'd had her breakfast, I had to help her get her clothes on. Setting things out for her. Doing up the strings on her corsets even. The buttons that ran in a line down the back of her dress. I didn't like the smell of her, just plain old-ish. I didn't like being so close.

"Girl," she called me.

She didn't even bother to find out my name. And, oh, she was serious about my training. She took me on a tour of inspection. She found fault with everything. I *had* to start over then. I was trying to do my best but her bell was always ringing. "I wish you to fetch my book for me." "I heard the mail. I am expecting letters. I wish them brought to me. There is a silver salver on the table by the front door for the purpose."

What was so *wrong* with me that I couldn't give her anything directly from my hand?

On it went and on. "Girl, do this," and "Girl, do that." "Girl, I believe I see a patch of dust." "Girl, your cap is crooked." Me with my "Yes, Madam" and "No, Madam" that seemed like the only answers allowed me. Me with my own attempts at the little curtsey bob.

By the end of the day my head was aching like there was a clamp around it. I wrapped myself in Mum's shawl over my nightie. I felt the feel of it but I still couldn't hardly get any sleep. Day after was the same—the same all over. I was getting so rattled. Worst of it was, the more rattled I got the more I was all thumbs and fingers. I dropped one of Cook's bowls. It fell to the floor and broke.

"Breakages come out of your wages," she told me.

Out of my wages? Wasn't what had gone to Mr. Alexander Brodie coming out of them as well? Did I even know what I was supposed to be getting? How was I going to be sending anything to Mum and Dad with all of that?

The panic that seemed like it was all that was left of me kept growing. Apart from anything else, I'd never been inside so much. The windows were all closed. The house was so stuffy. And I was so lonely. I'd no idea where Liz was even. I wasn't just lonely either. I was ashamed. I thought "the silent wonders"—Bessie and Mary—even they must be doing better than I was.

"Only old housework," Sarah had said. I'd gone off so bravely. I'd been such an idiot.

A week! A week almost. The uniform didn't seem so tight any longer, like maybe I'd shrunk inside it. And still there were the steps to be scrubbed every morning and the breakfasts and the lunches and the dinners and Mrs. Toms with her coughing and Cook not being pleased with me.

I was at the washing up again, the water in the tap still spurting. I dropped a plate. Not one of the good ones—the ones that I was sure cost more than I could imagine. Still it was another breakage.

"For goodness sake," Cook said. "Are you soft in the head or something?" I thought I must be. "You go on like this, you'll be out on your ear," she told me.

Out on my ear? Where would I go?

A morning came when Cook got called upstairs herself. "Menu day," she said to me.

Menu day? When she came back down, she brought a message. The message was that I was to fetch Mrs. Toms this thing that was called "a hansom cab." I felt my face go blank. My whole being. What was a "hansom cab," for heaven's sake?

"Where would I be finding that?" I asked.

Cook had her back to me. Apparently menu day was when she found out what food she had to be ordering. She was in

a hurry, checking in cupboards, writing a note to be sent
to the grocers.

"They're all lined up in the Haymarket. You must have passed
them on your way here," she got out. "Straight down Rennie's
Mill Road, the road you came by, where you're living. Down
onto Prescott Street," she added, lifting down some sugar. "Be
quick about it. It's today the cab's wanted, not next week."

That was it. I might've been glad to be outside but I didn't
know where I was going. Those directions Cook had given me.
She hadn't said right or left. "Down" though, "down" she had
said. I could see where the road was dropping. Down I went.

It was the smell of the sea and the fish guts growing
stronger as I got nearer to the harbour brought the picture
of the seal from home into my mind, I think. Soon as I thought
of her I could see her. I was sort of back there on the rocks.

I wasn't only seeing her. I was remembering the story.
How me and Dad had talked about it. How it had saddened me.
Thinking about the stealing of the skin. How the maid who'd
had that skin taken from her couldn't learn the ways of the land
at all at first. How even when she did, she must've felt so bad.

That's me, isn't it? I thought to myself. I'm just like her. I'm
all filled up with being where I shouldn't be. That's why I'm
making such a mess of things. That's why I don't know what to do.

My heart sank to my boots. I got this dull lump inside
of me. I'd stopped paying any mind to where I was going by
that time. I was breezing past all sorts of whatevers, running
almost.

Running because the water was calling to me. The water,
the sea.

All of sudden too, there it was. I'd made my way through
that crowd of people that was working there. I'd gone out onto

52

one of those great wharves. I was standing above the waves and the greyness, looking out.

What was I thinking? I'm not certain. I just know a head popped up. It wasn't the seal from home. Of course it wasn't. I might have been going daft but I wasn't daft enough to believe that, although I did find myself letting out a bit of a gasp.

"How did you get here?" I almost burst out.

They were so alike, the same size almost. Had to be a her too, didn't she? I could at least allow myself that.

I thought I should try to shoo her off. I thought it would be a dangerous place for her. I did sort of flap my apron at her. She took no notice. She dived and came up again. She seemed to be staring at me like she was trying to tell me something. Like her eyes were two great pools of darkness I could dive myself right into there and then.

I'd been wrung through with feelings of God knows what all. Now what I had was anger flooding into me. Black, black, black. Who was he, Mr. Alexander Brodie, to think he could sell us? To think we didn't matter? To get us uprooted? To be dropping us about with never so much as a by your leave?

Him and his little round hat there? I'd have smashed it onto his head if I could've. I'd have run at him with my own head down. I'd have punched him in the gut. I'd have shown him what for. I'd have let him have it.

Him that had tricked us. Stolen us, as good as.

Getting my hands on Mr. Alexander Brodie wasn't going to find the hansom cab I was supposed to be looking for though, was it? Mrs. Toms and her orders were coming back to me.

"What am I going to do?" I asked the seal.

She dived again. Again she poked her head up. "Look at me," she seemed to be saying, proud as punch.

That made me think how the seal of the story—she hadn't forgotten who she was. She cried and she cried in the beginning, but she kept on searching. Years went by but as soon as she found her skin, she went down to the beach with it. She pulled it on her. Even after all that time it still fit. She could plunge into the waves. She could swim and swim. She could join her own kind again.

"If she could manage, I can. Is that what you're trying to tell me?" I asked.

The seal in the water didn't answer. I didn't expect her to. Like I said, I wasn't completely daft.

The seal in the water simply dived once more. This time she came up with a fish in her mouth.

"She had to learn though, didn't she?" I murmured. "She had to learn the things of being a wife."

With that, I found myself sighing. My thoughts of discovering Mr. Alexander Brodie's whereabouts and attacking him, of leaping onto some boat and having it take me wherever it was going slipped away.

I'd felt like we were on our own—me and the seal there— but we weren't, of course. There was someone yelling at me, asking what I was doing in fact.

"Use the brains God gave you." That was a saying Mum had.

I'd come through a crowd. A crowd was people. So why didn't I ask one of them to help me? Soon as I turned I saw there was this woman, carrying a basket like the Atterley women did. I went up to her and she smiled at me. She didn't hesitate. She was ready enough to point me out the way.

"You'll know the Haymarket because there's hay there," she said with a laugh to me. "Hay is for horses, now isn't that it? Horses for the hansoms that carry folks where they're going."

"You'll know the Haymarket because there's hay there,"
she said with a laugh.

I got a glimmer of understanding. All I had to do was retrace my steps. I could've kicked myself for missing what was so obvious first time through. I mean hay is hay and the cabs weren't exactly tiny. Still, if I'd noticed them, I wouldn't have seen the seal, now would I? I wouldn't at all.

Next thing was to go up to one of the cab drivers. I had to be somewhat bolder with him because although I managed to get out he was supposed to be going to Rennie's Mill Road I realized I didn't know the number.

"You're to take me so I can show you," I said.

Of course, Cook wanted to know why the whole thing had used up rather more time than it was supposed to. I have to admit I lied. I said there hadn't been any cabs ready. I'd had to wait for one. I could tell from the look on her face she didn't believe me, but I also got the feeling she wasn't unhappy with the idea I might have a bit of spark.

I can't exactly explain why after that my "training" went better. I just know that it did. I was still working like a slave but at least I was doing my job properly. There wasn't any more splattering water all down my front! Not that Mrs. Toms didn't still find fault with everything.

Cook offered me a touch of comfort on that one. "She'd find fault with the angels if you want to know the truth of it," she said.

Cook now—I was getting the idea we might be more like allies, comrades on the battlefield, or some such.

I asked her about my wages. I told her about Mum and Dad depending on me. She said that's how it had been for her when she'd started in the city. Apparently she'd come from some little place as well. I'm not sure how she did it—especially seeing there were other things I was to pay for that Mr.

Alexander Brodie had omitted to mention. Like the uniform that didn't fit. I just know she made some "arrangements" so that what I had to give up was spread out over a longer time.

I told her how my uniform was tight. It was better but it was still pulling at me. She said there was an old one I could take a piece out of to let into a seam. I could sew it on her sewing machine. I did that. I found I could move more like myself again.

Here's a thing too. I discovered I was supposed to get an afternoon off every second week. There was a butcher boy came for deliveries. I reckoned if anybody would know where Liz was it would be some boy. Sure enough he said he'd take a note for me. We managed to get our half days off the same day.

Turned out her experience had been a little better than mine, but not so very much. Anyway the half days off gave us a chance to explore around so we weren't such strangers to the place. We even discovered the whereabouts of Bessie and Mary. They were still together, still not saying anything, so we didn't trouble ourselves any more with them.

One day I found myself making Cook a cup of tea, out of the blue when it wasn't time for it, because she looked tired.

"My Lord, girl, I reckon you'll do," she said to me.

That night in bed when I wrapped Mum's shawl around me I remembered there was a part to the seal story I hadn't thought about. I heard it—there in my high-up bedroom—in Dad's voice. How when the seal was being a wife she had children and with the children by times you could've thought she was happy.

I could think I was happy, couldn't I? I didn't have to stop knowing Mr. Alexander Brodie had treated us badly. I didn't have to stop being certain Mrs. Toms' dealings with me weren't right.

But I was who I was. When it came down to it, that couldn't be taken from me. I could think I was happy because often and often that's how I felt.

A place to live in this square sort of a box sort of a building
that was called a tenement. Streets upon streets of them.

Ninety Times
as High as the Moon

There was an old woman tossed up in a basket
Ninety times as high as the moon
Where she was going I could not but ask it
For in her hands she carried a broom
"Old woman, old woman, old woman," quoth I
"O whither, O whither, O whither so high?"
"To brush the cobwebs off the sky."
"Can I go with you?"
"Aye, by and by."

There was a surprise! Having that old rhyme come into my
mind as I was lying so quiet. In my bed, in New York City,
if you can believe it. New York City, of all the places I'd never
imagined I'd see. I was doing a bit of a think to myself in the
darkness. Not that the thinking didn't have its difficulties.
The bed was a narrow sort of a pull-out and I had to keep
as still as I could manage so I wouldn't wake Norah that was
beside me sound asleep.

Norah now, she was the daughter of my landlady, Bea Trimble. It was Bea who'd got me going there. She'd written Cook a letter. The letter had said Bea was looking for boarders. "Good girls, nice girls, with English so I can talk to them," was what she'd put. She'd gone on about how she had an apartment. How there'd be "a world of opportunity."

Bea was Cook's niece. Who was I to doubt her? After more than a year, I was fed up to the back teeth with slaving away for Mrs. Toms in her great house anyway. Truth to tell I'd been thinking of going back to Atterley. I fancied the sound of "opportunities" and "apartments" though.

I went to Liz on our day off. I gave her her chance to come with me. I thought she'd be eager but there was some cousin of someone or other who'd showed up in the household where she was working. He had an eye for her. It was all she could think of.

"Right," I said. "I'm not stopping. I'm going alone."

I was pleased with myself for that. I went to the harbour. I found a trading boat that would carry me. I was better at cities by then, of course. Bea had sent her address. I paid a boy to show me—clutching my little carpet bag again. I'll admit just the bit of New York I'd landed in made St. John's look as if you could put it on a postage stamp. Still I found where I had to go without too much fuss.

The old woman in the basket? She was a memory from a long time back. Sitting at my desk in the Atterley schoolroom, turning the page in my tatty old reader with its torn, worn edges. Coming to the picture of her, unexpected. Staring at it, figuring out the words that were written underneath it, touching that picture even. Going back to the same page over and over because she seemed like such a wonder—*Up in a basket*—her and her broom.

Years ago, and all of a sudden clear as day!

Why had she come to my mind? I asked myself. Norah turned over, tugging the sheet. I knew then—remembering like I was doing—it wasn't so strange. After all, I'd seen another wonder that very day, hadn't I? It was what I'd been thinking about.

She might not have been up in the sky but she was just as much of a puzzle, walking down the street through the pushing and shoving of me and everyone. All of us pouring out from our work places in the factories and the sweat shops of the "garment industry" where we toiled away.

Appearing out of nowhere. Coming up behind me, singing full on, for heaven's sake. A song the like I'd never heard before. Lovely so I could still feel the tingling it had sent all through me. Soaring so I wanted to yell out for the whole great crowd to be silent so they could hear.

Not that yelling was possible. I'd been struck dumb. On she'd come and on, carving a path for herself. All I'd wanted as she got to where I was was to go after her, to have more.

Yes, I was tired. Seven thirty in the morning we clocked in at the Global Shirtwaist Factory, which was my bit of churning out the blouses seemed like everyone in all the world was wearing. Eight in the evening it was by then. The hours weren't any better than they'd been at Mrs. Toms. I was tired and I was cold. It had been November when I'd arrived in New York. We were into March, but there was a raw dampness to the air still. We only had the one break in all the day and that was at lunch time. I was hungry as well.

Tired, cold, hungry. I'd forgotten it all. I'd up and left Angelika and Rebekkah that I was traipsing along with, that worked on either side of me. That were the same age as me, that were my best friends.

Oh whither, oh whither.

It was like the old singing woman was pulling me—her and her music. Something else I could see in my head as I lay in the kitchen there where our bed was. I'd gone through all the stir around me like nothing else existed. Passing folks that were selling their wares from carts in a thousand or so languages—the languages I knew by then belonged to the people of the Lower East Side where I'd come.

How could I attend to any of that? I'd been too caught up in listening. I'd only wanted to follow her. I'd wanted it that the music would never end.

So how was it she'd got away from me? How was it I'd lost her—disappearing completely—so that try as I might there was nothing for it but to give up and head back here to Bea's.

Bea's. Where was that now, you might ask.

No problem answering. Bea's was like everyone else's. A place to live in this square sort of a box sort of a building that was called a tenement. Streets upon streets of them. Hundreds and hundreds all filled up with apartments, all of the apartments the same. Bedroom, kitchen, and sitting room running into one another. That and nothing more.

It'd been something of a stunner, finding I'd be sharing a bed again. Discovering I wasn't in for quite the splendour I'd been dreaming of. Not that Bea didn't keep the place nice enough. I knew if I turned on the light I'd see everything spic and span and shining, all the pots in their right places, a little plant on the window sill, doilies on all the surfaces. Bea was good as Mum for that.

I wasn't going to be turning on the light though, was I? I'd caused enough trouble for one night. Coming in late so Bea had had to keep supper waiting, so the little ones—Belle and

Amy that were four and six—were teary and grizzling.
Not hardly lifting my fork up, I was so filled with wanting
to share the news of what I'd come upon.

I tugged the sheet back. I was angry still with Norah for
what had happened next. I'd have loved to give her a good
sharp poke, not enough to wake her, mind you, just to disturb
her a touch.

The thing was the words were hardly out of my mouth.
I hadn't really got started.

"Do you think I didn't see her? Do you think I don't know
she's crazy?" Norah had burst out.

I should have guessed how it would be with her, of course.
She who was so strict and straight always, never a giggle, even
if she was only eleven, not into long skirts yet. Her braid pulled
back so tight I sometimes wondered if it hurt her head.

A lump swelled up in my throat. I thought how I'd wanted
to argue. I knew why I hadn't. It came into me again as I shifted
in the bed the small amount that could be managed. How I'd
had this feeling, if I argued, the music would be hurt.

"You're as loony as she is," Norah had said to me later.

She'd whispered it in my ear when I was putting Belle
and Amy to bed where they slept with Bea in the bedroom.
I'd taken that task on so Bea could get back to the sewing
of buttons that was her contribution to the Needle Trade that
ruled us all. Piece work she did at home with every button
counting. Stitch, stitch, stitch.

Norah was into the dishes. What was the matter with her?
I wondered. How could she believe anyone who could make
such beauty could be mad?

It occurred to me a kick might be better than a poke but
I wasn't going to lower myself. I turned right over so I had my

back to her instead. We slept head to toe. It was the only way there was room for the two of us.

I was getting a bit distracted. It was hard not to. There was this air shaft thing in the apartment. We had our bed against it. It brought sounds from above us and below. Coughs, snores, quarrels. The worst was the little girl on the second floor that seemed to spend most of her life crying.

Crying wasn't what I wanted. I wanted that old woman.

Ninety times as high as the moon.

It was like when I'd seen her she'd opened up a patch of space in me.

How could she have done that when she was so ordinary looking? Her in her old grey coat, with her old woman's hat set firm upon her head. She just had. That was all there was to it.

Norah and Bea hadn't understood about her. There were others though, weren't there? Surely Angelika and Rebekkah wouldn't be like that. After all, *they'd* been my friends from the beginning.

Norah let out a small moan. I reckoned she was dreaming. It came to me maybe I could give her feet a tickle. I was sixteen though, wasn't I? I should be looking after her.

Still....

Fact is she didn't want me there. She wasn't nice to me. Sure, she'd brought me to stand before Mr. Spengler that was the boss of Global's sleeve room. She'd made it so I could get considered as an operator on the machines. She'd wanted to be rid of me though, hadn't she? She'd hightailed herself off to where she worked—with the other kids at the table at the back—as soon as she could.

It was Angelika and Rebekkah who'd shown me how to get my machine going with my foot on the knob on the floor.

It was Angelika and Rebekkah who'd taught me how to snatch up the fabric that was sleeves cut out ready—the basting threads set in where the seams were to go. They'd shown me how to hold those sleeves so I could get the seams stitched straight. They'd explained to me how we'd get paid by the sleeve bundle that the boy brought to us. They'd helped me learn to do the bundles fast. They'd taken me round, they'd introduced me to Paolina and Rachele so we could go about together. They'd brought me to their homes to meet their families. They'd taken me to dances. We'd giggled together like Liz and me had—about certain boys. Other girl stuff too, clothes that we fancied.

It didn't seem to matter we had to do a fair amount of bowing and fiddling around one another to figure out whatever it was we were saying. Me with what I'd been forced to realize was a way of speaking didn't belong anywhere except on the Island. Them with their English they'd had to learn.

Yes, yes, I thought to myself. I'll speak to them tomorrow. The old singing woman—if I explain, they'll see how I felt about her. They'll see why I left them. They won't want to miss the delight of her, not really. We can look for her together. Yes, yes, yes. I'll talk to them about her as soon as I get the chance.

Lunch time that was, the machines with their great thread spools—the bobbins—silent and turned off. All of us with our chairs pushed back, from the rows and rows we worked in, enjoying our bit of freedom, stretching ourselves as best we could.

Me with my bread and lassie that was what Bea gave me like Mum would have, Rebekkah with what I'd come to learn was called a bagel, Angelika with a sandwich with some kind of sausage in it I wasn't sure I liked.

Turned out they'd heard her. They just hadn't paid any mind.

"Do you know what language she was singing in?" I asked them.

"Was not Yiddish! Was not my language!" Rebekkah said. She had this look on her face told me she was proud of that. She had the same thing in her voice.

Rebekkah wasn't much of a one for words. Angelika was the talker. She let out this stream. "It my language. It Italian. It opera like they have in my country. Like my papa sing on Saturdays when he shaving to go out. Like my mama love to listen to."

"So didn't you like it?" I asked her.

"Why she singing in streets?" Angelika answered.

"What difference does it make? It sounded so lovely."

"Not to me. To me it just make us seem like we all crazy. We Italian people. Like we got nothing better to do than go wandering around."

Crazy! There was that word again. I was flattened.

"I hope she not come again. I hope she not come again ever."

Could it be I was wrong? Could the old singing woman not be anything so special? I let the thought come into me, but I couldn't get myself to believe it. Not anywhere in me. Not, for certain, when she came back.

That was Saturday when we got out early. We were lined up. Outside this nickelodeon place where they showed the moving pictures, women tied to railroad lines with trains coming to run over them, horses galloping, the piano being played so loud.

This time her song was different. It was sadder. It brought tears to my eyes.

"I'll just be a minute," I told the others.

Again I lost her.

When I got back to them Rebekkah raised her hands up to her face. She wiggled her fingers. She made her eyes go scary "Maybe she a wi-i-i-tch," she said to me, drawing the word out.

Angelika laughed. Paolina and Rachele joined in with her. They did the hand thing too.

"Was witch in my village. My mama tell me they all frightened. All the children, adults even," Paolina said.

Ninety times as high as the moon.

The old singing woman was no witch. I was sure. She couldn't be. Again and again I followed her. I have to admit as time went by I was tempted to plead with the others. To tell them they didn't know what they were missing, to ask them to give her a try. I didn't do any of that. I figured if they couldn't hear what I heard, then they couldn't. Nothing more to say.

I have to admit I took my fair share of teasing for going after her. Wasn't just the other girls either. I'd get back to Bea's to Norah putting her finger to her head and making that sign you make when you're really doubting whether someone's stunned. I can't pretend I didn't care. I can't pretend it didn't hurt me but I wasn't about to stop.

More and more, too, I thought how brave she was—the way she went about there, letting all that she wanted come out of her. Having it flowing around.

Always—it was like some sort of cobwebs were being brushed out of me. Maybe I wouldn't have thought of that. It wouldn't have occurred to me. But our world was so dusty. Something from the sleeve room I've not said about. How there was always lint from the fabric hanging all about us, getting into our noses and into our throats.

Funny how you get caught up in your own world. I was so fretted about being the only one who cared, it didn't come to me to notice I wasn't. The old singing woman had been appearing and disappearing a while before I ever clapped eyes on Zeke.

Soon as I did I saw from the way he was walking he was following her, just the way I was. Had been most like from the start. I knew him because he was a puller, at the table at the back with Norah and the other kids. Taking out the basting threads after us operators had done what was needed to get the sleeves ready for the next step, which was sewing them onto the bodices on the third floor above. A bit of a wild thing, always getting himself into trouble, darting hither and yon the slightest chance that came. Norah didn't like him. She said he was dirty. It's true he needed a haircut and there were holes in his pants and his sweaters but I got the feeling whoever he had for a mother wasn't like Bea.

I'd never minded anyway. I didn't for sure when I saw the look on his face. The same look I imagined probably was on mine.

"You like her too, don't you?" he said to me.

I nodded.

"I think she's magic," he whispered.

It wasn't what I expected of him. I felt a little thrill. I saw he had this penny whistle he was pulling out of his pocket. He was starting to finger the holes as if he was trying to make the notes she was lifting so bursting up to the skies.

"Can you give us a tune?" I asked him, after she'd gone from us.

"Not the way she can," he answered

"The tune you can give is all I'm wanting," I told him.

He put the whistle to his lips. He wasn't that good but
he played with something of a flourish I was pleased to hear
in him. He put a mischievousness to it. I set a couple of cents
in his hands. He grinned at me and bent himself forward
in a cheeky bow.

We were in league after that. We'd wait for each other
after work sometimes. We'd go searching. You'd have thought
we might have talked about what we were seeking that meant
so much to us, but we didn't. We neither of us had the words.
We did talk of other things. Zeke wanted to know about where
I'd come from. He wanted to hear about Atterley. He seemed
to like to see it in his head. He told how he was the same as me.
He had a lot of brothers and sisters. He was the oldest boy and
I was the oldest girl.

So it went on and so it went on and then the weather grew
warmer even though the old singing woman was still wearing
the same old clothes. All around folks got into sitting out on the
balconies that were on top of all the fire escapes that went up
outside those tenements.

At first I was enjoying it—being outside more—but
as the days went by I got to feeling there was some sort
of tightness that had come upon the scene. First thing I noticed
was how people in the sleeve room were with their bundles.
Like they were grabbing them, guarding them almost. Like
the bundles were something to be kept secret, something
to be stored.

It got worse every day. There wasn't the same chit chat any
longer. People were quarreling. I was afraid to look at anyone
else sideways. Angelika and Rebekkah even. A Saturday came
when I suggested we might go to some dance or other. I was
given head shakes like I was a kind of a sinner. Bea got into

getting at me and at me to be putting more of my money aside "in case."

"What's going on? Why's everyone so touchy?" I asked Angelika at last.

It was the start of the day. We were in our places ready. Her eyes went wide. She put her hand to her mouth. "Edie, I so sorry," she burst out.

"Whatever for?" I asked her.

"You, me, Rebekkah—is like we've known each other always. Me, Rebekkah—we should think how you just get here. How this your first year."

"What's that have to do with it?"

"It have to do with how we should have told you. It have to do with how we should make sure you know."

"Know what?" I was getting desperate. The machines would be turned on any minute. Felt like I'd never find out.

We had one more minute. Angelika used it, making the words come quickly. "Summer is not so much work. Season getting to be over."

Over? But we'd been so busy. Sleeve after sleeve going under the machine needles. Our fingers numb. Our backs and necks like they could break with aching. Bundle after bundle. Seam after seam so I'd been cross-eyed with it. Hadn't we all of us? Hour after hour after hour.

How could you have a season on shirtwaists anyway? Weren't seasons for berries? Weren't seasons for fish?

Rebekkah had been listening. "Short time is coming," she put in.

Short time? Didn't matter whether I could get my head around the idea or whether I couldn't. They were right. May got into June. Mum's letters were full of how the capelin were

72

coming in, of how the fishing was shaping up nicely. Mine were all about how the warmth had turned to heat so thick you could hardly move a muscle without reducing yourself to a puddle of sweat.

I didn't tell her the rest of it. Step one—a drop in our pay per bundle so we were working the same but taking less away at the end of the week in the packets with our pay. Step two— Mr. Spengler saying we'd be finishing the next few days at five o'clock.

Not long before he was treating us like working till five was a privilege, announcing it wasn't going to be five any longer. It was going to be four. Four, then three, then out at lunch time. Me thinking how at home there was always stuff we were growing—potatoes, carrots. Fish we were catching, fish of some sort. Food that didn't have to be bought.

"What's next?" I asked Rebekkah.

"No work at all," Rebekkah said, shrugging her shoulders, shaking her head.

Cruel thing was we got let in. Half an hour we were kept sitting there idle, so we could be told our "services would not be needed." We were getting "a little break."

"What about our money?" someone shouted.

Because it was Friday. We might not have worked much that week but we'd not done nothing. Saturday was when we got paid.

"I fear your remuneration is out of my hands. It is a matter for the owners," Mr. Spengler said. Like that wasn't a problem, like it wouldn't matter at all.

A couple of the older women started weeping—ones with children, I imagined. Mostly we simply pushed our chairs back, got to our feet. When we were down the stairs and outside, we stood for a while on the street without saying anything. Not just us, mind. It wasn't only Global that was "closing temporarily." The same was happening all over. Took us a while to start drifting off to where we lived.

Turned out Norah and me were spared from having to tell Bea about it. She knew already. She'd had no jackets for the buttons that morning. No one else that worked from home in the building had had anything in the way of sewing either. They were all of them—the women—standing about around their doorways, looking so sad and grim.

Bea shed a tear or two when we came in. As she was drying her eyes she looked at me, "I shouldn't have got you here, now should I?" she burst out.

World of opportunities! I can't say I hadn't thought the exact same thing myself. Quite often, in fact.

She blew her nose. "Always seems maybe we're through with it, maybe it won't happen this year," she went on. "I was so dragged out too. I wanted to have someone who wasn't so strange to me. Someone I could trust with the little ones."

Didn't seem much point doing anything but tell her I understood. She'd started gathering up the blankets before I'd hardly got the words out from me.

"Where's she going with them?" I asked Norah.

I got one of Norah's eye rolls for my pains.

"We're not cold, are we?"

"What's that got to do with it?"

"She's putting them in hock. She's taking them to the pawn shop. She thinks if she gets there before everyone else does she'll be given a better price."

In hock? What was that? I suppose my bewilderment was obvious.

Norah's lip curled. "It's where they keep stuff for you. They give you a bit of money and a ticket so you can get it back later, only then it costs more. It's like a loan, but different."

In hock was something I was going to find out about all too well. Awful, taking things in—Mum's shawl even, finally. Her shawl that, of course, I'd brought with me. That I cherished. Having to argue and bargain over what you'd had your hands on, what you'd used and looked at and felt. Everything going we had no immediate use for. Not the little plant. Plants had to be looked after. No, it was those doilies that Bea was so proud of, the picture she had from the Island that hung on the wall. The pots she didn't cook with often. Our winter coats. Our gloves, our winter woolies.

The apartment was getting barer on a daily basis. Spaces staring back at us. Same thing at Angelika's, same thing at Rebekkah's. Same all over, far as I could see. Me and Norah combing the alleyways for whatever we could find in the way of wood for Bea to light the stove to do the cooking. Oatmeal morning, noon, and night. Just the odd bit of something else to add to it when Bea could wheedle it out of the man who sold the meat, the man who sold the vegetables, the payment going "on the slate."

I did write to Mum about it finally. I had to. I needed to tell her I couldn't be sending her anything. She sent me money instead. It was my own. She'd been putting it away to have for later.

I was shamed to get it, but not so shamed I thought to send it back. Not with the little ones getting paler and quieter. Norah too for all her toughness, despite the number of times I saw Bea pushing her food in her children's direction, eating so little herself.

Rent day was the worst. We'd be sitting in the apartment. We'd hear the rent man knocking on the doors. We'd hear the voices, our own neighbours trying to save themselves.

"You'll not be putting us out on the street."

"You know us."

"We're giving you as much as we've got. We're going hungry."

The knocks would be nearer. We'd know our turn would come.

Week after week it went on. Thing I know clearest is how I hated it. How I didn't want to be sitting about with nothing to be doing. I didn't want to be in the middle of all the wretchedness that had fallen on all of us tenement people there.

Week after week and the old singing woman never appearing, not even once. I looked for her and looked for her. I can say that for certain. I can say too—us with no work… I thought she'd left us. I thought we were letting her down maybe. We weren't good enough for her any more.

Truth to tell, I'd decided it was hopeless. Finally, finally I'd given up.

For sure and certain she wasn't in my mind the day there was this little tap at the door in the middle of the morning. A little tap when Bea was drinking a cup of tea that was weak as water, and me and Norah and the little ones were doing I don't know what.

Bea now, she had her ways. She liked to answer the door herself, even if Belle and Amy were always clustering about her skirts when she did it. Up she got then, out of her seat at the table. I saw it was Mrs. Tocher that was Jewish like Rebekkah. That lived above us. Mrs. Tocher that'd come. She looked like

being there was the last thing in the world she wanted
to be doing.

"Is little girl," she got out. "Little girl Sheena, we hear
crying."

My stomach turned over. I felt sick. The little girl who
cried and cried—she'd not been crying, had she? Not the last
few days. I'd noticed, but I hadn't known what I was noticing.
I'd just had the feeling of something missing.

"What's happened to her?" I blurted.

"She dead." Mrs. Tocher wrung her hands.

Dead? But all she'd had was unhappiness.

"Was it her mother came to tell you?" Bea asked.

I was wondering the same, seeing as how everyone said
the mother never spoke to anyone. She hardly came out of
the apartment. When she did it was like she was in a daze.

Mrs. Tocher shook her head. "So quiet there I push open
door. See mother sitting with baby, no moving. Why she not
come to me, that lady? I help her."

Seemed like Bea wanted to sit with her head in her hands.
That's not what she did though. She took off her apron.
She sighed.

"Norah, you're to look after Belle and Amy," she announced.

"There's things to be done," she went on.

"That why I here," said Mrs. Tocher.

I thought of my Janie. My Janie that I'd saved. My Janie that
Mum wrote about, that was talking nineteen to the dozen.
That I'd had the thrill of.

I realized I hadn't even know the little girl's name until
now. I'd never even seen her. Surely I should've gone down
there. I should've, but I hadn't.

Bea was at the door again already.

"Best be at it," she muttered.

They went together, those two women. I heard them going down the stairs. I heard what they were saying. The sounds came up the air shaft.

"Hush now. Hush. We have to take her."

There was this awful wail. Norah clutched Belle and Amy to her. She stood there, holding the two of them, like they'd needed protecting. Protecting from me?

"You won't be able to pay your rent, now will you?" she spat out. "I know Mum'll say she'll wait but if you can't pay your rent we'd be better off without you."

The words stabbed at me. I'd been worrying about the self-same thing myself. So, Bea had got me there under false pretenses. So I'd been useful to them. I wasn't going to be useful any more, was I?

And Belle! Belle and Amy! I loved them. Bea too. And even Norah, really.

All I could think was how I should get out of there. I grabbed my hat up and I went.

There was this small park not so far away. It was dry and dusty, filled with blowing papers. Still I knew there were benches there so that's where I took myself. I sat myself down trying to figure out what I should do next.

I can't say I was having much luck getting to anything in the way of an answer when I caught sight of Zeke. He was leaning with his back against this tree. I hadn't seen him in ages.

"What are you doing here?" I asked him.

He was looking more raggedy than ever. I could see he didn't want to tell me but he'd decided he would anyway.

"It's where I sleep," he said. "There's others. There's a lot of us."

"You sleep *here*, in the open?"

"We do all right." He tilted his head back.

"So where's your family?"

"Dad has rules. For me it's if you don't bring money, you can't come home. If Mum tries to let me in, he hits her."

"Oh my Lord," was all I could think to say.

"I can feed myself. I've got my whistle. You don't have to feel sorry for me."

Sorry wasn't what was needed. I realized that. Zeke perched himself beside me, drawing himself up a bit.

"Have you seen the old singing woman?" he asked me.

All I could do was shake my head. I was still shaking it when we heard her. She was by the park's edge. Doesn't seem believable, does it? That's how it was though. And oh, the song that was coming out of her.

I could've laid that little girl that had died down at her feet there was so much to it. It was like she had in it all our troubles. And all the anger that was coming in me again. Everything we were going through. And the seal woman coming to me.

All of it, and hope as well.

Zeke and me, we looked at one another. I thought I saw Zeke tremble. I felt a shiver down my spine. She stood for a moment before she started moving on again. She was still in her old coat and her old hat, hot though it was.

Singing and singing and singing.

"We'll not lose her this time," I said.

I was on my feet already.

O whither, O whither.

Zeke was standing up as well.

Seems strange but it was as if she was leading us. Block after block we walked. At first the blocks looked the same as those we were coming from. Worn out, if you can say such a thing about buildings. Tired to the bone.

Then they weren't the same any longer. There were all these fine ladies and gentlemen, riding in cars and carriages wearing lovely clothes. Stores with jewels in the windows—diamonds, rubies, emeralds—dresses such as those fine ladies would wear to balls.

"I said she was magic, didn't I?" Zeke whispered. "I reckon this proves it."

Sights such as we'd only heard tell of. Sights such as I'd never seen—not even in St. John's. We wanted to stop and look. It was like the old singing woman knew that, like she'd brought us where she wanted to. Poof! She was gone.
No, I don't mean *poof*. Not really. But still, we were on our own there.

Seventh Avenue we'd come up. Seventh Avenue we stayed on.

"Do you reckon we'll ever have stuff like this?" Zeke asked, his nose pressed against the glass of some place that sold men's clothing.

"You never know," I answered.

He gave me a grin. "Be all right, wouldn't it?"

"Fancy schmancy!"

I suppose it was afternoon by then. We'd tried keeping to the shade but we were boiling. Didn't stop us. There weren't any stores any more. We'd come to this place where there were great big pillars, making a sort of gateway.

"Can we go through, do you reckon?" Zeke asked me.

"We can give it a try," I told him.

So we did. It wasn't what we were expecting. It wasn't at all.

"It's like what you said about, where you come from," he got out.

We came to where there was a lake with boats on. They were being rowed by people who looked as if they were doing it for fun.

It was too, sort of. No sea, of course but green—green all over. All this wide spread grass. Great humps of rocks even. Trees that were big, their branches spreading like even I had never seen.

Zeke was standing gazing as if he couldn't believe it.

"You can run if you want to," I told him.

"Yes," he said. "I can."

He did as well. He ran with all his being. He spread his arms wide like he might fly.

"There's room," he said when he got back to me.

Then he was off again, scrambling up some rock face.

"When you told me about all that space I couldn't imagine what it would be like," he got out.

It was grand to see his face so shining, his eyes so lit up bright. Not that I wasn't plain and simple bowled over by all of it, just for myself. Felt I'd finally got some fresh air in my lungs.

"This is the best day of my life," Zeke told me.

We came to where there was a lake with boats on. They were being rowed by people who looked as if they were doing it for fun. Wouldn't that give Dad a chuckle? I thought.

Zeke was all agog. There was a heron. It was standing in the reeds the way they did by the brook in Atterley. I made sure he noticed.

"You want to look at the bird there," I told him.

Ninety times as high as the moon.

"How could anything be so not-moving?" he demanded.

Couldn't go on forever, could it? Had to get down to the everlasting problem.

"I'm kind of hungry," Zeke muttered, in the end.

He was. I was. We'd come so far. I reckoned neither of us had had what you might exactly call breakfast. I didn't know what to do. I didn't have any money. Zeke wasn't waiting for me. He was getting his whistle out. He was climbing up onto another great rock chunk. He was putting out a tune.

There I was again, not knowing what got into me. I mean, I was aware of how you were supposed to behave in public. I still lifted my skirts up and started doing a jig. I thought it was just him and me. I could see folks strolling but I didn't think any of them would pay us any mind. It came as quite the surprise when I realized there were these five children come to watch us, children that were clapping with the beat.

They started dancing too. Zeke was enjoying it. I could tell from how he was playing better than I'd ever heard him. Faster and faster till he'd got what in Atterley we'd have called "a kitchen party" going, only it was in the outdoors there, the children holding hands in a circle, swinging round and round. An older man with a cane came up. It was clear he was with them.

"Grand," he kept saying, his eyes getting brighter every minute. "Nothing like music for having fun."

I was a bit nervous. They were all of them dressed so well. They looked like their clothes had come from the stores we'd seen on our journey there. The man had a vest with a watch chain even. He had a beard that was trimmed so neat.

I knew I ought to be embarrassed but I couldn't manage it. I was too busy doing some of the fancy steps I knew.

"You are a tribute to the power of Central Park," the man said, when no one could go on any longer, when Zeke and me and the children were all too tired.

Central Park? I thought to myself. Is that where we've come to? I suppose it must be. Central Park that I believed I might have heard of as one of New York's prides. I was proud enough too. It seemed to me we'd done well for ourselves. We'd given some pleasure.

"Your names are?" the man said.

"Zeke," Zeke answered.

"Edie Murphy," I put in.

"Miller. Mr. Miller."

The man shook hands with us. I found myself doing a little curtsey like I'd learned at Mrs. Toms.

"No need for that," he said.

He reached inside his jacket. He took out his wallet. It occurred to me all of a sudden I'd turned myself into a street performer. I hoped Zeke wasn't going to tell anyone. But how could I not be glad about the money?

"Half each?" Mr. Miller asked.

We nodded. He paid Zeke first. I thought how Zeke could go to his home if he wanted to. I found myself with a full week's wages being put into my hands. I felt the tears prick. I had some trouble holding them back, I'll tell you.

"We're very grateful," I said, trying to be as polite as I knew how.

We were going to go on our way but Mr. Miller told us we shouldn't. He told us the children were his grandchildren. He introduced us. Adele and Mattie, Robert and Richard and Nan. He said they'd come out for a picnic. He said we should join them. So there we were, all of us sat round this white cloth. Rolls and ham and hard-boiled eggs and cheeses. A couple of different kinds of them. A cake even. Cookies. Plates to eat off, knives and forks.

The children were giving us the odd glance like they weren't too certain. After all, it wasn't a usual sight—us and the rich folks at the same table, even if the table was on the ground. Mr. Miller seemed happy as a clam. He kept urging us to eat as much as we liked. I had to give Zeke a nudge now and then to stop him grabbing at stuff. Not that I wasn't tempted to do some grabbing myself. It was all so good. Even when we'd eaten our fill there was lots left over. I saw Zeke eyeing it.

"Why don't I give you the remains of the feast to take home with you?" Mr. Miller suggested.

I didn't know how to tell him how much those "remains" were going to mean. I could see even Norah's face lighting up. I could imagine the relief in Bea. And at Zeke's place…or with the boys he slept with…

Can I go with you?

Had the old singing woman known this might happen? Was there really something of magic in her? Had Zeke been right about that? And who was this Mr. Miller fellow? Was he a saint or something? There were stories, weren't there, about saints coming to earth to be with people. Where had he come from? Why was he bothering with us?

He was another wonder, wasn't he? Another thing I couldn't explain. Seemed like the world had more than I'd imagined. Although a bit I was afraid. It occurred to me all of a sudden—the old singing women, her being such a mystery. She could have come to us from Faerie. Zeke and me—we could be in some sort of dream. We could wake up and find the wonder taken from us, everything changed and gone.

We could, but there was Mr. Miller saying, "I suspect you've come a long way. I suspect you've walked here."

He seemed so real. He was rich. But as well he was ordinary. Kindly.

There was nothing for it but to nod.

"I'll have my carriage take us home and then carry you back," he went on.

Talk about icing on the cake. Next thing I knew we were off to where the carriage was waiting, on this road with trees hanging over it. Once we'd all climbed in, the driver gave a flick to the reins. The horse was incredible. Its head so high. Its coat so shiny.

I guess the children were getting more used to us. The one that was Robert asked if he could try Zeke's penny whistle. They all of them tried it in the end. We got to this house that was enormous. We stopped there. I wondered what the children's mum and dad were going to think about what had happened. I wondered if they were going to get told.

"It's been a pleasure to meet you," Mr. Miller said, when they'd all climbed out.

We watched them go inside. Zeke and me were looking at one another, shrugging and bewildered. Bedazzled?

"Where to?" the driver asked us from his seat in front.

I wasn't quite sure what to answer.

"Lower East Side," Zeke spoke up, bold as brass.

"That's a long trip," the coachman grumbled.

"Hard on the feet," Zeke told him.

I thought we'd get dropped off near where we were. I thought we'd get shouted at to get lost. Sure enough though, the driver did what he been told to. He took us all the way.

I'd like to say we came home in triumph. We did get quite a crowd out being as how it wasn't exactly usual seeing the likes of us in a carriage of that kind in those parts. There was still that dead little girl though, wasn't there? Her body was laid out properly by that time. Bea and Mrs. Tocher had seen to it. The mother was still sitting. It was as if she hadn't moved but she was silent once more. I'd have liked to give her Mr. Miller's money for something more than a city burial but how could I when really that money was going to belong to Bea?

At least I had something to offer. I had my share of the food from the picnic so there could be a bit of a wake. Wasn't just us at Bea's that got some in the end then. There was others from the building came by.

I had the food and I had the day we'd had—me and Zeke there. That mattered. I was sure it did.

Zeke now, he took off. He didn't say where he was going and I didn't ask.

The big surprise was Norah. "I'm sorry," she said to me, like really she meant it.

I was quite taken aback. Still, I thought maybe she'd be beginning to trust me, seeing us how I hadn't gone off with my "riches." I hadn't set to spending it on myself.

I thought maybe things might be a bit different between us. I knew I'd like that. I knew I'd be happy enough to be with her as if we were family, like I was with Winnie and Tess at home.

I never did see the old singing woman again.

Somehow I didn't expect to, although I would have loved to thank her for what it was she'd done. She was such a gift to me. Her music came to me often. I wished and wished the others—Angelika, Rebekkah, Bea, Norah, the whole of the Lower East Side really, all of us workers. I wished and wished everyone had understood.

There was an old woman tossed up in a basket
Ninety times as high as the moon
Where she was going I could not but ask it
For in her hands she carried a broom
"Old woman, old woman, old woman," quoth I
"O whither, O whither, O whither so high?"

Ninety Times as High as the Moon

"To brush the cobwebs off the sky."
"Can I go with you?"
"Aye, by and by."

I taught that rhyme to Belle and Amy. They loved it just like
I had—Belle especially. She took to asking me "oh whither"
when I was going out the door. She'd climb into the laundry
basket bringing the broom. I told her she was getting to be
quite the "quother." I wrote to Mum to make sure she'd pass the
words on to little Janie, although I was pretty sure Janie would
come upon that same old reader when she went to school.

*I was just bending over my machine there, back at Global, caught
in all the noise and thrumming of the needles going up and down.
Row upon row of us same as usual.*

Our Voices Raised

Was it because of the old singing woman I did it? I can't tell you. I just know there was this stirring inside me and the words came bubbling up. "*Sing, sing, what shall we sing?*" A silly song, one Bea sang to Belle and Amy when they were getting troublesome. So she could shift them into enjoying themselves instead of quarreling and teasing each other all the time.

I know, too, I had no thoughts in my head of anything coming out of it. I was just bending over my machine there, back at Global, caught in all the noise and thrumming of the needles going up and down. Row upon row of us same as usual. Work begun again. Fall season carrying itself onward in that great room.

I never thought Angelika would give me a nudge as I got into the second line, which was even sillier—"*Granny's old petticoat tied up with string.*" A nudge so I'd sing the first line over, "*Sing, sing, what shall we sing?*"

That's how it was though. Next thing I knew out of the corner of my eye I saw this wicked kind of a smile come to her face. Next thing after that she was opening her mouth like she was answering me, only she was making what she was singing louder so the sound would go further.

Some think the world is made for fun and frolic,

And so do I! And so do I!

It was a song I knew. Everyone was always singing it. Didn't seem right to let her go at it alone so I joined in.

Some think it well to be all melancholic,

To pine and sigh; to pine and sigh;

Beside me, Rebekkah lifted her head up. I thought she'd tell us to "shush." It wasn't only she didn't talk as much as Angelika. She was more nervous when it came to following Global's rules.

No shushing from her that day.

But I, I love to spend my time in singing,

Some joyous song, some joyous song,

There we were then, the three of us. A voice rose up to join us from the row ahead. I'm not sure whose it was because already there were others catching on to what we were doing.

To set the air with music bravely ringing

Is far from wrong! Is far from wrong!

By the time we got to the chorus just about everyone was going at it,

Harken, harken, music sounds a-far!

Harken, harken, with a happy heart!

Funiculì, funiculà, funiculì, funiculà!

Joy is everywhere, funiculì, funiculà!

Talk about joy. We were all of us laughing. Angelika started in on the second verse only she was giving it out in Italian. That's the language she'd said the song was made in. She'd said it was really about some railway carrying folks up some mountain. She'd told me it was something else her papa sang when he was shaving on a Saturday night.

What did the rest of us care about her papa? She and the others that were from Italy could sing in their own language if they wanted to. We were going on in English, loud as we could.

Ah me! 'tis strange that some should take to sighing,
And like it well! And like it well!

We'd have kept at it, only the power went off. That meant our machines stopped. Mr. Spengler came out of his office all in a rage. He stood in front of us, his face as red as a beetroot. He was shaking almost he was so angry.

"There will be no more of this," he thundered. "We will have no more singing at the Global Shirtwaist Factory."

A murmuring and a muttering went round.

"Come on," someone called out. "We were working faster."

"It true," Paolina yelled.

It was too. I'd felt it in my hands as they pushed the material along, getting the stitches into it. The room had been shaking almost with the speed of our machines. Not that it didn't shake most times. But it was shaking more.

We were late into the afternoon. Weary part of the day. Thursday when all of us were wondering how we were going to get through the rest of the week. Dragging a bit with being so sure we had to do it, however we might feel.

"I will brook no disobedience," Mr. Spengler ranted.

With that he was off and going back into his lair.

"Old goat," Angelika mouthed at me.

"Rat face," I mouthed back.

The whole room full of us were taken up with "sighing" then. The power was put back on again. I reached out. Felt like my arm had gotten heavier all of a sudden. I took up the next sleeve and the next one.

Weren't we like machines, almost, ourselves? Each sleeve so close to the one going before it, the one coming after. Just a quick snip with the scissors needed to cut them apart.

I didn't have to look round. I knew there was every one of us feeling the same way. Bundle after bundle after bundle. No end to them.

But the song had been so good. The song had given us spirit—for "our labours" even.

Wasn't only Mr. Spengler that was angry. It was me. I wasn't just angry either. I was boiling mad. Madder than I'd been at Mr. Alexander Brodie when I'd stood there by the sea in the harbour even.

That stirring I said about, the stirring inside me. It was a new thing I was finding. A thing that came from all the meetings me and Angelika and Rebekkah had been going to in little dingy rooms. Meetings we'd come out of with our heads filled with thoughts we'd never dreamt of. Words about how we were forced to be working. Spoken by these men and women who kept talking about something called a "union."

"A shame upon humanity."

"A black mark upon our country."

"A sin in such a time."

That's what *they* said "our conditions of employment" were.

The needle jammed. I was getting myself in a lather. Probably I should be replacing it. The needle, I mean. The trouble was when I put a new needle in I had to pay for it. I don't think I said about that before. Pay for new needles. Pay to use our machines even. Another thing the speakers in those meetings said wasn't how it should be.

We shouldn't be paying for anything, they said. After all,

where would the owners be without us? After all we had
our rights.

A bit of singing. Surely we had a right to that? Made me
want to throw my head back. "*Sing, sing, what shall we sing?*"
Made me want to belt it out again. I couldn't though, could I?
Did I really want my wages cut? Did I really want to lose
my job?

Still I wasn't quite beaten. I went for a bit of humming
under my breath.

Welcome, sisters, to our number
Welcome to our heart and hand.
At our post we shall not slumber
Strong in union we shall stand.

It was the song we sang always when the meetings were
beginning. It was only the tune I was doing, mind, but Angelika
heard me. She gave me a nod. She slipped her arm in mine
as we were going down the stairs when at last the day was over.

"You wait. We not stopping," she said to me.

Turned out there were others felt like us. We moved off
a-ways so Mr. Spengler wouldn't come down to find us
gathered. Reen even that was from England. Reen that was
so old she walked with a cane. Paolina, Rachele, maybe a dozen
or so. Norah among them. A dozen or so at least.

"We got to keep going. Is not just for us, is for girls at
Triangle. They so courage," Paolina let out, when we were
far enough off to think we might be safe.

Triangle meant Triangle Shirtwaist Factory. Those
that worked there were in our thoughts a lot. We stopped
in a huddle on the corner where there was this cart with
bits and bobs of jewellry. We'd all got pictures in our heads,
most like. The girls at Triangle leaving their stations, "withdrawing

their services." Who'd have thought such a thing was possible? "Strike" being a word that hadn't come into our lives before.

Strike. It was exciting. It was unbelievable. The Union was "negotiating" with a lot of the owners about it. They were getting the "demands" all properly listed. Simple things really. More air. Less crowding. As if we might be human beings! That wasn't the end of it either. The Union was saying everything should be all organized so there'd be none of that end of the season nonsense. Work should be regular. We shouldn't be driven to it all the hours God sent us, then have nothing. Something else too—we should know exactly what was in our bundles so we weren't always getting cheated of our due. One more thing I haven't said about. One more thing that wasn't "right."

The wicked look came to Angelika's face again.

"Is big—the sleeve room."

Wasn't difficult to guess what she was meaning. Hardly time to catch our breaths and there were suggestions coming from all over, although we were keeping our voices down, being careful still. Avoiding the tattletales we knew went about.

"Mr. Spengler—he not be everywhere."

"Not all at the same time."

"One starts where he not…"

"Others follow when can do it."

"Others stay silent."

"Keep him hopping."

"Make him dance for us."

"Not us alone."

"We too few."

"Have to get everybody."

"Each to tell someone."

"Lot of someones."

That was it. We had a plan.

"Is time to go home," Paolina announced finally.

"Got to go home, so can come back tomorrow," Angelika added.

There was a bit of a cheer. First time ever. Cheering for another sleeve-room day!

"*Sing, sing, what shall we sing?*" I set forth as we were parting.

I heard more than one "*Funiculì, funiculà*" come drifting back.

Even Bea had sort of a chuckle when we told her. Not that she wasn't worried. We all were. Still...

"Giving the owners a run for their money," Bea said. "I never thought I'd see the day,"

Norah and me—we were doing better with each other by that time. It was like I'd hoped. She'd got into talking to me when we were in bed at night. She'd told me about how her dad had taken off on the family. She'd told me about the folks they'd had as boarders there before. Bad lots, some of them.

She'd not been to the meetings. Bea hadn't let her. I'd filled her in as best I could. At first she wasn't having any of it. She was bound and determined she was getting on as an operator sometime. She wasn't letting anything get in the way of that.

Still, the more I talked, the more she listened. Lately she'd been drinking in every word.

"Those Union people—do they really believe we can make things better?" she'd asked me over and over.

Felt like she was becoming a bit of a firebrand.

"I don't want it—Belle and Amy being at some pulling table.

I keep hoping they can get to read and write like you can," she whispered to me that night before she went to sleep.

I reached up and found her hand under the covers. I gave it a little squeeze. I held her words to me. Belle and Amy, Belle and Amy. Was there even a school they could go to? Had to be, didn't there? Had to for sure.

Still it was another time of lying awake in the darkness. At the start, I was all filled up with excitement. Didn't last long. I couldn't help it. I found myself thinking about what a strike might mean when it came to us not getting paid. Feeling again how the apartment had been so bare that awful summer we'd just gone through. I remembered about Bea's doilies. How it wasn't much more than a couple of weeks since we'd been able to fetch them back.

Made me realize getting everyone going the same direction wasn't going to be easy. I mean, there must've been others doing what I was. Mulling on what having no work brought.

The Union said we had to stick to our course. We had to steer straight. But there were those night-time noises pulling at me. Noises made by people. The sound that wasn't. Sound of Sheena, that baby, the one who'd died. Her mum gone somewhere else. Four men I didn't like passing in the hallway in that apartment now.

Steer straight. Keep to the plan.

Yes, yes, we had to. We had to or we'd lose ourselves. That's what I decided.

I made sure Norah and me were early for work the next morning. I took my chance when it came. "*Sing, sing, what shall we sing?*"

I'm going to have to admit it—in the beginning our voices were all too thin. There were those that had been part of us standing there on the sidewalk, dreaming the whole thing up, that were too nervous when push came to shove, let alone others.

"Maybe not so good idea," Angelika muttered a couple of days later.

It was Reen that made the difference. Reen, by getting caught. She was such a warbler. You could tell how much she loved to sing. She had guts too. She took the lead as often as she could manage. She was into *By the Light of the Silvery Moon* that day. I could see Mr. Spengler bearing down on her.

"Reen," I whispered, loud as I could, but she didn't hear me. Not in time, at least.

He got her by the shoulders. He shook her. She tried to push him off with her bent old hands but he was too strong for her. That did it. Rebekkah started into this thing she told me later was called a *nigun*. Wasn't just the Jewish girls set in with her, even if it was in Yiddish. After all it became clear soon enough all that was really needed was a lot of "yaidle-eidle-ei."

We could do that, couldn't we, every single one of us? We could and we did. The music coming in waves, like we'd figured it'd have to. Everyone catching on to how that could be managed. Little winks and nudges going round the room. Norah and the pullers joining in even, soon as they got the chance. The older ones anyway. Not the younger ones.... They were just too little. They couldn't understand.

Every day after that, we'd have something going some time. Music the organ grinder with his little monkey brought us; *She Was Only a Bird in a Gilded Cage*, *You Are My Honey Honeysuckle*, *Yankee Doodle*, *Hello My Ragtime Girl*. *March of the Tin Soldiers*, even, with its "tiddley-om-poms." Mr. Spengler rushing hither and yon. Hiring himself a couple of assistants he was so determined to catch us. Him and his bright red face.

Sounds easy, doesn't it? It wasn't. There was always a fear in us. We'd been bullied so long. We were so used to obeying. We were getting more and more determined though. I could feel it. I could hear it when we talked about it end of the day.

"Mum, Mum, you should've heard us," Norah said, often and often when we got home.

She'd sing our songs for Belle and Amy. I'd never heard her singing. News came to us the Leierson Shirtwaist girls had followed those at Triangle. They'd walked off the job as well. More news. There were sweatshops finding themselves with nobody showing up, the small dark places that were the worst for everything.

We'd pass girls picketing everywhere we went. I should say about that, I think. How "girls" was a word we used for ourselves. It was a word we were proud of, a word that held us together, even though some of us were beyond "girls" when it came to age. Reen, of course, but all sorts of others. Still there were so many of us that were younger. Me. Angelika, Rebekkah, Paolina, Rachele. So many of us that were not even twenty yet.

And how else would we call ourselves? Wasn't men that were filling those great sewing rooms, was it? It wasn't. Wasn't at all.

Those that were picketing—we'd call out to them. We'd wish them luck. Couldn't last forever—"the situation"—now, could it? Not with us being so ready. Not with the owners, the bosses paying us no mind.

"Never heard such nonsense," Mr. Spengler said to us, one morning when he took it upon himself to congratulate us that we were still at our work.

There we were again, boiling mad and looking at one another. Nonsense? Nonsense! That was our lives.

The singing went on. The meetings got bigger. Those little dingy rooms—they couldn't hold our numbers any more. Other places had to be found. It was like we were holding our breath, like we were breathing properly for the first time ever—both things the same time.

Couldn't last. Just couldn't. There was one great, huge, enormous meeting. It was at this place called the Cooper Union Hall. Norah did go with us to that one. Bea actually insisted.

Not that we could get in. There were just too many. We had to stand outside with messages being passed to us. Getting translated because most of what was happening was in Yiddish. I'll say that now because it's the truth of it. It was often those of them that were Jewish that were at the fore.

"There's a girl."

"Coming to stage."

"Look like she been beaten."

"Don't matter. Girl say enough talk."

"Girl say we all have to get in on it."

"Girl say we have to have strike that is general."

That girl. That girl we couldn't see, we could only be told of. That girl was calling for what we at Global wanted, what we were yelling our hearts out in support of. A strike for all of us. Yes, and yes, and yes.

I don't think any of us slept hardly a wink that night. I know me and Norah didn't. We were just too taken up with hopes and dreams. How maybe Norah could go to school herself. How maybe Bea wouldn't always have to be working at the buttons. We could get another bed even.

"Wouldn't that be something, having your toes out of my earholes?" I said to her.

"Spreading myself out, not having you grab the covers," she shot back.

By then it was November. Dawn of a clear, bright morning. We knew what we were to do. We'd learned all about it. We were to go work but we were not to go in. Imagine the talk. Imagine us all standing there outside the factory, clustering about the door. A lady came—a Union lady, wearing this sash over her shoulder. ILGWU. International Ladies' Garment Workers Union that stood for. I saw tears of joy come to Reen's eyes at the sight.

International Ladies' Garment Workers Union. We'd paid our dues by then. We were members. ILGWU. We belonged.

That lady—a fine lady. She got up on the steps so she could give us the rules for how we'd be picketing now ourselves. You could have heard a pin drop. We were so eager to do what had to be done and do it right. Angelika and me, Rebekkah, Norah, Rachele, Paolina. All of us, all of us. Nodding in agreement.

We were to keep moving, we mustn't block the doorway. We mustn't be in groups of more than two or three. We weren't to reach out or touch anyone we wanted to talk to about what we were doing. We were just to walk alongside them.

Other stuff, too, that I'll get to later. Big thing we had to understand was the rules weren't made up by the Union without good reason. The rules were so we'd "stay inside the law."

"I have more factories I must visit," the fine lady said when she was finished. "Remember though, come dressed in your best. There will be photographers. They will be taking pictures for the newspapers."

In a pig's eye, I thought to myself. I didn't just think it. I said it aloud. Caused me a bit of trouble, that did. It was the language thing mostly. I had to explain what I was meaning, Norah and Reen being the only ones who'd been able to get it right straight off.

Out we stepped. I took Reen's arm. I knew with her I was going to be walking slowly. I decided slowly didn't matter. After all, I had a pretty strong feeling she was always hurting. I thought maybe I could take the weight of her a little. I could help.

End of the block and back again. Over and over. All the hours of it. Over and over again.

In a pig's eye! Showed how much I didn't know, now didn't it?

Before we went home that evening, there was Zeke among us, his eyes so shiny I thought they'd burst out of his head. He'd given up on the pulling. He'd gone into the business of newspaper selling. It suited him better—him with all his darting about.

"You've got to look. You've got to see," he yelled at me.

He was holding up this newspaper. He was showing me the picture on the front page. Strikers! Girls like us with sashes on them. Girls in a line. Over the picture a headline: **UPRISING OF THE 20,000.** I dug in my purse. I paid him so I could take that paper in my hand.

"Listen to this," I called out.

So what we weren't supposed to be stopping? Everyone had to hear, didn't they? Of course, they did. But I'd have to read it out. There were those in plenty had no chance for school like I'd had those years in Atterley. Those whose English wasn't good enough too.

I read it out, loud as I could, my voice shaking with
the splendour of it. How we were making history.
We were the first strike of women here in America.
We were "an inspiration," "a signal to the downtrodden masses."
Who were they? I wondered. Seemed like a strange phrase
to be using but I didn't bother about that.

Twenty thousand. *Twenty thousand*. Who'd have thought it?

We went back to our walking, our picketing. We passed
each other, our faces mixed up with amazement and with fight.
There was a bit of "*funiculì, funiculà*-ing," and other songs
to be singing under our breaths.

Things happened after that I'd never imagined. We kept
talking about it to each other, saying how it was amazing. Bea,
Mrs. Tocher, Reen, Rebekkah, Angelika, Rachele, Paolina.
Everyone.

I mean there were letters coming from all over the country
to support us. They were pinned up in the Union "headquarters"
in this Clinton Hall place. Where the Union had rooms, where
there were always women working at tables, sorting out what
needed sorting.

Wasn't just letters, it was money that was pouring in.
Money so we could have something in the way of strike pay
to look after ourselves. Pay we'd all been so worried about.
So there could be food for the families. Soup kitchens set up.
The money was being given by rich people. I couldn't hardly
countenance it after Mrs. Toms.

We all of us had sashes by that time, same as those fine
ladies that worked with us, organized marches for us. Sashes
or signs to hang round our necks that told anyone who cared
to be looking what we were about. Signs that had **Strike**
written on them.

Striding we went, row upon row upon row of us—
20,000—not round the neighbourhood. No, we went where
me and Zeke had gone in the summer. Uptown with thousands
coming into the streets to cheer us. Thousands standing all
along the sidewalks, every step of the way.

No doubt in us by then. No doubt we were changing our
world. Seemed so obvious, didn't it? All of us out there.
The owners would have to listen to us. The owners would have
to give in.

What did we know about their deep, deep pockets—stuffed
with money they'd made off our backs? How was it to occur
to us—didn't matter how many factories we took ourselves out
of, the bosses could fill them up with scabs?

Dreadful women. Brawling and horrible. I'd watch them
as they got brought in. All in a crowd together, laughing and
taunting at us. I'd wonder who was going to be sitting at my
machine—that I kept clean, that I looked after. I hated the
thought of it.

That was nothing though—not compared to knowing how
they were being given our wages. Here's a thing too. The police
were in on it. They were getting money from the owners
as well. I wouldn't have thought it possible. It was Reen who
found out about it. She brought the information to us in
a newspaper the Union itself put out. A paper named the *Call*.

The police said it wasn't true. Made sense though, didn't it?
Why else was it there was no help from the police for the
members of the ILGWU? Why was it the police were guarding
those scab women, making sure those scab women got in
Global's doors? Every other factory the same thing.

"Protecting the honest citizens of New York," we were told
the police chief said of what they were up to.

"So we not citizens? We not honest?" Rebekkah got out, when we heard.

I wanted to answer her but I couldn't. I mean what answer was there? All I could do was shake my head.

The scab women kept coming.

"Do you know there's a strike on?" we called out.

That was all we were allowed to do. It was one of those other picketing rules. We did our best "to be calm," "to be quiet," "to maintain our dignity," like the Union told us, but the cops came in among us. They kept pushing and shoving us this way and that. Thugs the owners hired too.

We went on singing our songs—under our breaths, of course. You could hear in the sound of them how much we didn't like what was being done to us. How much it hurt us. How much it riled us up.

Us in the cold that was biting. Rain, snow. Fingers, toes aching with the bitter, bitter slice of it. Us that had got locked out now.

The owners laughing at us, so it felt like. No, they weren't ready to be giving us more washrooms even! They absolutely weren't about to be considering some more standard wage. They were looking down their noses. They weren't "negotiating." The ILGWU kept trying. The ILGWU told us.

One week. Two weeks. There was a calendar at the Clinton Hall, the days ticked off on it. We were heading up to Christmas.

Morning I saw this cop come at Norah with his night stick—his great thick billy club—just because she'd stepped off the curb, I couldn't stand it any longer. I forced myself in front of her.

"She's just a kid. You leave her alone," I shouted in his face.

I was being grabbed by the arms and manhandled,
I was being carted away.

Didn't take more than a minute. I was surrounded.
I was being grabbed by the arms and manhandled, I was being
carted away.

There were others trying to come with me. Didn't seem
right though.

"Keep back. Keep out of it," I yelled at them over my
shoulder.

Not that I think it was me that stopped them. Who could
stop Reen with her cane there? Who could stop Angelika?

I don't think it was me that stopped them. I think that was
the cops as well.

I don't know. I can't be sure. Before I could gather my wits
I was in this police wagon, looking through the window, trying
to figure out where I was going. Not succeeding at all. Only
thing I could be certain of was we were travelling some
distance. It wasn't the cop shop round the corner where
I thought I'd be.

The journey seemed to take a long time. As we went, I tried
to prepare myself. I thought it all over. How I knew I wasn't the
first. It was getting to be regular. There'd been other girls from
other factories picked up. That girl that had spoken at the
Cooper Union Meeting—Clara Lemlich—that's how she'd got
those bruises we'd been told about. Those terrible bruises.

Still that had been in the beginning. Now things were more
organized. So—so I'd be put in a cell with a whole lot of
others. We'd all be together. I wouldn't really have to worry.
I'd only be kept there for a night. Something else the fine ladies
had taken charge of. When we were brought to the court
rooms in the morning the ladies would be there. We'd be
charged with disturbing the peace or some such. We'd be fined
but those ladies would pay what was needed to get us free.

"Calm, quiet, maintaining my dignity." I had it all worked out.

The wagon stopped. I stepped down of my own accord. I went into this building we'd come to as if nothing could shake me.

That's when it started. That's when I was put into this box of a cell, all by myself. Hour after hour I waited. Nothing happened. No one came. There wasn't even a bed or a chair. There was just the floor. I didn't know what to do with myself. I used the bucket in the corner to relieve myself. I had to, but it shamed me.

How would anyone ever find me there? I wondered.

The idea of being forgotten terrified me. By the time the door opened and some cop I hadn't seen before let himself in, I was a wreck.

"So you don't like billy clubs?" he said to me. Him in his dark blue uniform with its shiny buttons, him with his cap still on his head.

I did get some words out. "No, no, I don't like them."

They weren't much though. Not enough to make him think I was likely to be doing him any damage. Not exactly brave.

His billy club was hanging from his belt. He unhooked it, held it.

"Maybe you could do with some practice," he said.

He had this leer. He didn't hit me. He just began sort of prodding me, pushing me into corners, forcing me about the cell.

"Right," he said when he was finished. "I'll be back. You've not seen the last of me."

He kept to that promise, let me tell you. Seemed like hardly any time had gone by. There he was again. Prodding me in my breasts, in my private parts at the top of my legs, the parts

I wanted hidden. Behind, in front. Places I didn't know I had even.

Bruises were coming on me now. I could feel them.

Back and back and back. Always with something a little bit different. There was once he left the door open.

"You want to get out? You just go through there," he jeered at me.

I knew what was going to happen if I tried.

There was another time when he showed up with some buddy. They were both of them at it. Teasing, mocking.

"Doesn't she run well?"

"Isn't she lovely?"

Next he brought a whole crowd with him. They all had billy clubs. He pushed me outside the cell and put me in the middle of their circle. They sent me one to another.

"Keep her moving. Keep her moving."

I wanted to resist, to not be driven, but I couldn't. In the between whiles, I fell to whimpering, huddling in corners, trying to hide myself away. I didn't know whether it was day or night. I didn't know anything. It was like the world had turned to nothing. It was like him—him coming to get me—that was all there was.

I was certain it was never going to stop. Certain I was going to die there. Certain any minute I was going to wet myself. Certain he was going to hit me—maybe...maybe...now.

Oh, he was pleased with himself too. He'd look at me and he'd be all smiling. I wanted to throw myself at his feet and plead with him. I think perhaps I did. Kneeling, there on the floor, so cold and stony. Shaming myself again.

Never occurred to me I'd get used to it. Never thought it'd be a shock when I was told they were letting me go, dumping me off like I was some baggage.

Not a word of explanation. Nothing to say why I'd been treated how I had.

Where was I anyway? Was I in New York even?

Took me forever to get to some place I could recognize, my legs all weak beneath me. It was almost by chance I managed to reach the Clinton Hall.

Standing there, gazing about me as if I'd landed off the moon, I caused such a stir. Everything stopped. Everyone came crowding over to me.

"Do you need something to eat?"

"Would you like a glass of water?"

"What is it that has happened to you?"

Shows how bad I looked, I guess. A chair was brought. I sat myself on it. I don't know why it was so important to me but I had to find out what day it was, how long I'd been away.

"You're the one the Global girls have been asking about, aren't you?" one of the women said then.

"I suppose I am. I suppose I must be," I answered.

"Edie—Edie Murphy." Strange it seemed to hear my name.

"You've been gone three days," someone else said gently.

Was that all? I wondered. There was a buzz of talking.

"We'll send a message to tell the Global girls you're all right."

"To tell them they should come and help you."

"The girls at Global should be informed but we must get her home immediately." That was the one with the gentle voice again.

She had gentle hands as well. She helped me into a cab. She went up the stairs to the apartment with me. Did I tell her the address? I suppose I must have.

Bea's face went white as a sheet when she caught sight of me.

"We thought we'd never see you again," she said.

Then she was all a-bustle, thanking the one who'd brought me, pulling the bed out so I could lie down. As soon as I got on the bed, I started into shaking. Angelika, Rebekkah, Paolina, Rachele, Norah, Reen—wasn't long before they came to see me. They were all excitement to find me safe, pleased to pieces to have me back with them.

"So good you here."

"We so worried."

I couldn't hardly look at them. The shaking had taken me over. It was all I could care about. All I could hear was the chattering of my teeth.

"You're going to have leave her to me," Bea told them.

They went away disappointed. I didn't like that. But it was as if I was far away from them, as if they were talking to me from some other place.

The shaking went on. Bea wrapped Mum's shawl about me. Didn't do what it usually did. I'd got it back from the pawn shop soon as I could because it was such a comfort. Not this time. It was like it was some foreign object I'd never seen before.

She made me a hot water bottle. She brought soup for me to drink. She kept Belle and Amy away from me. She said I needed to be left in peace.

Norah came home—end of the day there.

"It's all my fault. I'm sorry. You saved me," she said to me.

Only thing I could do was tell her it didn't matter, although I knew that wasn't enough. She needed something more to let her know I wasn't angry with her. I didn't have it in me. I didn't have anything of anything it seemed.

Bea kept putting her hand to my forehead to see if I had

a fever. A fever wasn't the problem. I still kept shaking though. Even when Norah was there in bed with me. Wasn't till next morning I could hold myself still.

"You stay where you are," Bea told me.

I couldn't do much else. It was days before I could get back to the picket line. When I did everyone wanted to talk to me. They wanted to know what had happened. How could I tell them it was just a lot of prodding I'd gone through? How could I say about that?

Angelika, Paolina, Rebekkah, Reen, Rachele.

I'd been so alone in the cell. It was like I'd got lost somewhere. Like I couldn't let them find me. So they were my friends. So we'd had good times together. None of that mattered. I just wanted them to stop bothering me.

I took to walking by myself. They all had a try at bringing me back to them. I wouldn't let them in. Not even Reen. Reen, one wet pouring awful day, telling me how she'd had kids. How they'd been taken from her. When she wasn't that much older than I was. Reen crying even.

Old bitch, was all I could think to myself. Trying to prove she understands. What business is it of hers anyway? I hated myself for it. Still it's what I thought.

Christmas came and went. The year before I'd gone to sing carols at Angelika's, although the carols were all in Italian. She asked me to go there to her family again. I shook my head at her, like I was a dog shaking water off itself.

"They're whispering about you," Norah said to me one night in our bed.

"They can whisper all they want," I answered. Harsh and fierce.

"But they want to know what's troubling you."

"Too bad for them."

"I truly am sorry," she said to me.

I just turned my back on her. I didn't even have the grace to offer her a word.

Zeke came to me on the lines with a message. Zeke was always coming with messages. Somehow he'd got to be a Union runner. Him and his penny whistle. I think he was getting paid for doing the running as well.

"You're wanted at the Clinton Hall," he told me.

I was wanted so I went. Turned out there was going to be some great "rally." To celebrate the "bravery" of those who'd been imprisoned. I was supposed to be having my name put on a list. It was the lady with the gentle voice who told me.

"I was eager to make sure you did not miss this special event," she said.

I started to tell her I didn't think I should be included. She wrote my name down anyway. Name down or not, I made my mind up I wasn't having anything to do with it. Trouble was there started to be posters put up. Word got out. How we were to be taken in carriages. We were going uptown for this as well. To some Carnegie Hall place. How it was important. It was another way to prove our worth to our supporters. "To show them our mettle."

Everyone was all thrilled. They kept on and on about it. They found out the wheres and whens of how those of us that were listed should be meeting.

"We come. We help you get dressed—me and Rebekkah," Angelika said.

I tried to stop them but I couldn't. They were like steamrollers.

"I can dress myself," I insisted.

They showed up anyway. Angelika brought me a brooch
to borrow. Rebekkah lent me a bracelet with blue stones in it.

"Is my mama's. She want for you to wear it," she told me.

They wouldn't even let me go by myself to the meeting
place. They went with me. There was no escaping. They joined
the crowd that had gathered to wave us off.

It was well into January by then, an evening. The owners
still not settling, the strike pay getting thinner. Bea's doilies
back in the pawn shop. The doilies and other things. Mum's
shawl coming up on the list.

All I wanted—right from the moment we set out—was for
the whole thing to be over. The carriage that took us—there was
no one in it I knew, thank goodness, but I didn't want to be sitting
there with the others. Them that were so happy and proud and
pleased and chattering round about me. I just kept looking out.

I didn't want to be wearing the sash that said *Arrested* that
we were given when we got there. I didn't want to be where
I had to be sitting, up on that stage.

Three hundred and seventy of us, crowded together.
On display. The building so beautiful. A theatre, rows and rows
of seating. Balconies even. Fine, fine uptown people. Everyone
cheering. All of the seats jam-packed.

Mostly I didn't want to be listening to the speeches where
everything was made to sound so glorious.

"These girls with their unbreakable commitment."

"Their undaunted dedication."

"These girls with their bravery."

"The heroism that is theirs."

Hours and hours it seemed to last. When it was time to go
I couldn't stand it any longer. I went to the ILGWU worker
that had brought us. I told her I was going to get home on my own.

"Are you sure?" she asked.

I nodded.

"You can't walk," she insisted.

She gave me a token for the railway—the El. I tucked it in my purse. I didn't wait to see the rest of them leave, them with their sashes on still, all of them still congratulating themselves. I went in the opposite direction. I tore my sash off. I couldn't quite bring myself to throw it away. I scrunched it up though. I put that in my purse, too.

Where was I going? How did I know? Luck it was really brought me back to those pillars at the edge of that place that was Central Park. At first when I saw them I didn't want to go any further. I'd had such a good time with Zeke there. How could I darken that?

In the end though, I couldn't resist. I wanted the rocks to put my hands on, even in the darkness. I wanted the grass feel under my feet. The earth too—there'd be a smell to it, wouldn't there? I knew that smell. I'd recognize it.

Sing, sing, what shall we sing?

I hadn't taken more than a couple of steps. The words were in my head again. Only now they were mocking me. There was a bitter sharpness to them. I could taste it almost on my tongue. Tears came to my eyes. I started sobbing. I wanted to howl like a wolf but I didn't. I didn't want anyone around me. I didn't want to be calling attention to myself.

There were more tears. A great deep heaving in my chest. Worse than the waves on the ocean when it's storming—felt like. My hands up to my face. My fingers soaked so wet. Sobs that were racking me, rocking me. Tears and tears and more tears coming. Tears and tears and tears.

"No one can cry forever." I think that's a saying.

I guess that has a truth.

Seemed I'd got myself to a bench. Seemed I was sitting there.

What else to do? Only one thing really.

I got to my feet. I used my token for the El. So late by that time I was almost the only passenger aboard. The only one stepping out from the station. Almost the only one walking through the Lower East Side streets.

Was it out of the tears? The rocks and grass and earth around me?

How can I say? I just know the streets were different to me then. Like all those people in all those tenements—like I could feel them breathing. Like they mattered to me more. All of them—even the ones I thought were horrible. Even the scab women maybe? Maybe. Had to be some reason they were so desperate for the money, didn't there? My people anyway— the ones that were toiling away. Being good to each other mostly. Whether I knew them or whether I didn't.

The stuff I'd heard at Carnegie Hall felt different to me too.

So there were three hundred and more arrested—some who'd been sent to the Workhouse. But it could have been any of us. It wasn't nothing, simply keeping on walking the picket lines. Feeling we'd never be warm again.

Bea with her doilies, wanting the apartment to be a bit more than rough and ready. That wasn't nothing either. Reen— Reen losing her kids. Losing her kids and still trying to help me. Mrs. Tocher caring about Sheena and her mother.

Wasn't nothing I'd done, stepping in front of Norah even if after...

Thousands of tenements. Thousands of people. All of them sleeping. Hardly a one of them being certain where the next meal was coming from. Keeping on though. Doing what they did.

Mum and Dad too. My family in Atterley.

I didn't have that far to go, my footsteps echoing, but it was far enough for me to work out how it was time for me to be changing what I'd been up to since I'd been in jail.

I reckoned I'd have to go at it slowly. I mean, I couldn't just go back to being what I had been. The prodding was there inside me and it wasn't going to go away.

I figured I'd start with giving out a few hugs and see where I went from there. Turned out I didn't have to wait long to get at it. Turned out not everyone was sleeping. I'd told Bea not to wait up but she had. When I put my arms around her, she held me tightly. She didn't ask any questions. I was grateful for that. It meant I could let stuff out from me gradually, as it came.

On into March the strike lasted. The police kept up their harassment. Angelika got a night in prison, so did Paolina. They looked at me with understanding in their eyes and I made sure I gave understanding to them.

There were lots of places settled earlier, but not Global. The owners at Global hung on and hung on. The owners hung on and so did we that were the workers. We wouldn't go back without a contract and we got one at the last. I can't say things were a whole lot better when the strike was finished, but they were some.

The world hadn't exactly been turned over like we'd hope for. More like getting some door that had been jammed shut tight to open, even if it was only just a crack. After all, a crack you can put your foot in. Big thing was we'd stood up for ourselves. Big thing was we knew if we could stand up for ourselves once, we could stand up for ourselves again.

Sing, sing, what shall we sing??

We didn't get anything written into our agreement about our right to lift our voices up when we felt like it but we did keep at it. We sang when we wanted. There was no one could stop us. Not us, not likely. Not the girls of the second-floor Global Shirtwaist sleeve-makers room.

How could I not look up to see the flames that were leaping so fierce
out the top of the building?

To See the Stars

If ever there was a time I wanted to block my ears and cover my eyes, it was then. I was longing to run. Hide. Shut it all out—the awful, awful realness of it. I wanted to believe it wasn't happening. I was making it all up.

How could I though? How could I even think not to listen to the sobbing that was going on around me?

"My Chiara, she in there."

"That my Magda."

"My Fredele."

"My Heneh."

The dreadful screaming that was getting itself repeated, over and over, and then over and over again. How could I not look up to see the flames that were leaping so fierce out the top of the building? Not have every bit of my whole being fixed on the girls that were crowding out onto the window ledges? Crowding with nowhere else to be going, for the fire at their backs?

"Don't jump," people were shouting.

What else were they to do?

Horrible—to watch them, throwing themselves
out into the emptiness. They were eight floors up, for God's
sake. Nine, ten some of them. They must have been so
desperate. They must have known they hadn't a hope in
all the world.

But their clothes were on fire. Their hair was burning.
I could feel the heat from where I was on the ground even.
So what must that heat have been like for them?

In ones and twos they came.

"Don't jump."

"Don't jump."

"Don't jump."

Some of them were holding hands with each other.
For strength? For friendship?

How should I know? I just know it was them—those
girls—that were tumbling, twisting. Falling, falling, falling.
It was them the screams were coming from. Wretched high
wails I'd never imagined I'd hear from anyone's mouth,
let alone someone that was just like me.

Running we'd gone there, holding our long skirts up, not
to be tripping. The usual gang—me, Angelika, Norah, Rebekkah,
Rachele, Paolina. Saturday early let-out. Saturday time to be
glad. Giggling down the stairs, talking, planning. "What we
going to do this evening? Where we going to go?"

Down the stairs into that breath of smoke sting that was
on the air already. We'd hardly even set foot on the sidewalk,
we'd hardly had time to smell it, when everyone that might
have been standing about and chatting was charging off the
same direction.

"There's a fire."

"There's a fire."

"There's a fire."

We didn't even know where we were heading. Not in the beginning. Then the words came.

"It's at Triangle."

That made us run faster.

"They get out late always at Triangle," Angelika puffed.

It was Paolina said the other thing. "They shut in. Doors locked on them, Triangle workers."

Faster and faster still.

What can I say of the sight that met us? The top of the building was where the Triangle rooms were. I'd been there—a couple of times—for errands. It was plain. There was no denying it. The top of the building was where the fire was.

I could see the girls, the women on the window ledges right from when we got there. I could see the fire crews. I could see the water being sent up from the hoses. I could see the ladders. Ladders that weren't long enough.

"Don't jump."

"Don't jump."

"Don't jump."

The firemen had nets but the nets didn't seem to be catching anyone. Each time someone jumped there was a hard, hard *thunk*.

"Look," Norah cried out.

"Oh God, God, the fire escape," Rachele yelled.

My heart skipped a couple of beats for the thought there was safety for some of them. Twenty? Thirty? Forty? Was that really how many had come out there?

I should have known. Those fire escapes. They were so flimsy. Always shaking when there was just a couple of us on them. The fire escape was crumbling. It was tearing itself off the wall. More screams were rising. More were falling, trying to grab at something, anything.

"My Rosa."

"My Mary."

Maybe I did cover my eyes, but it was only for a moment. In that moment it came to me how every single girl I could see had her coat on. Every single one was ready to leave. A couple of minutes more they'd all have been out of there. They'd have been standing where we were. They'd have been alive.

That's when I thought, too, about the panic. When it ran all through me. The pushing and shoving that must have been among them. The pounding at the doors. Doors that wouldn't open. Locked doors. The fear, the fear, the fear.

Another one and another. Seemed like it was going to last forever. Wasn't very long though, not really. The firemen were still at it with their hoses. There was all sorts of fuss and bother but there wasn't any jumping any more.

Took us a while to stop gazing upwards. Me anyway. It was only when I got hold of the fact there really, truly wasn't anyone else going to get out. That's when I looked at those I'd come with. That's when I saw the horror in their faces, the horror I knew was on my own.

It's when I looked round too. When I realized how big the crowd was. Hundreds. Thousands. All of us standing there. Nothing we could do.

"We marching with Triangle workers," Angelika said.

She didn't need to. I reckon there wasn't a one of us wasn't remembering those times. Wasn't a one of us hadn't a picture in her head of some face. Faces more like. Faces in plenty. Voices as well. Words spoken between us. I shuffled my feet. I stared at them.

Beside me I felt this movement. I was surprised, finding it was Norah getting in closer, reaching out to take my hand. Pleased enough to be doing something for her, though. Pleased enough to have her near.

No, "pleased" isn't the word. There wasn't any pleasure in anything. How could there be in that moment? How at such a time?

A cop was calling out through one of those bullhorn things.

"We are asking you to go to your homes. There is nothing for you to do here."

There was a bit of stirring but it was people pushing forward.

"My Anna, I got to find out."

"My Sarah."

The cop went on. His voice was blurry but I managed to make out what he was saying. I heard how he was telling everyone that the bodies of the dead were to be taken to some police station. The people that had been pushing forward started pushing back. Space was made for them. Paths opened.

"Triangle a shithouse," Paolina burst out.

I'd never heard her speak like that. Still the only thing I could think was she was right.

Norah moved closer. She was leaning against me almost. She was holding my hand so hard it hurt.

The cop kept doing his best to be getting everyone away from there. We didn't even discuss the matter. Our group. We just went on standing, like everyone else. Sometimes we talked a bit. Mostly we didn't. Reen came pushing and hobbling through the crowd.

"I didn't want to be on my own. I wanted to be with folks I work with," she told us.

"We so glad to see you," Rachele said.

Only bit of gladness to be found.

Hour after hour. There weren't any flames any more, although there was still smoke. Hour after hour with firemen doing whatever it was they were doing. Wagons coming. Wagons with horses. Vans with engines. Coming. Going. Taking the bodies away.

"They'll have to be identified," a man that was near us muttered.

"Now, there's a job you wouldn't wish on your worst enemy," another man muttered back.

Hour after hour. I thought the whole of the building would come down but it didn't. It kept on towering above us. We kept glancing up at its great height. Mostly though we'd got our eyes fixed, trying now to see what was happening on the ground.

The longer we stood, the more scraps and snatches of news came floating round us. How it was only on the Triangle floors there'd been anyone left working. How everyone else had gone home.

How it was true—what it seemed—the fire hadn't been anywhere but at Triangle. It hadn't burned down further. How there were survivors. The fire hadn't taken everyone. There were some that had got out through the doors at the bottom, some over the roof to the next building. On the other side, where we couldn't see.

How what that man had said, about the "identifying." It hadn't hardly started. There were so many. So many.

Didn't take more than the thought of that. The screams were in my head again. The falling. Falling, falling, falling.

Took a while but gradually more from Global found us. More from the sleeve room came to be where we were. Other rooms as well. Didn't matter who came, Norah stayed close like she was glued to me. Like I was some sort of lifeline for her.

More and more from Global. Then there was Zeke. Looking like I'd never seen him. All the spark gone out of him, biting his lip hard, his cheeks so pale.

"Have you been here from the beginning, Zeke?" I asked him.

He nodded.

"You've seen it all then?"

"I was with the other paper boys. I wanted to find you though."

Him that was shuffling his feet now. Him that was looking at his boots. I put my free arm round his shoulder. I felt how thin he was. Not a bit of spare flesh on his body.

"It's horrible, isn't it?" he murmured.

"Horrible. *Horrible*," I said.

Hard to believe the crowd was still growing, but it was. Angelika's mother arrived and Rebekkah's papa, some cousin of Rachele. All sorts of bits of people's families. A miracle, how we came upon each other, but we did.

I started worrying about Bea. It was a long time after we should have been home. A longer than long time. A few more minutes and we'll go, I kept thinking to myself. A few more and a few more, piling one atop the other.

Then she was coming at us, battling her way there, pushing people aside. Her face was red. Her hair all over.

"What the devil do you think you're up to?" she yelled at us. "Couldn't you at least have sent me word."

Hadn't thought of that, now had I? I didn't know what to say. She looked so shook up. She seemed so angry. Norah was cowering against me almost. Norah, the firebrand. Norah so straight.

Only a minute, Bea sighed. All the anger drained from her. She shook her head—at herself it seemed like. She put her arms out. She drew Norah away from where she was by me. She held her like she wanted to keep on holding her forever.

"As long as you're all right. That's all that matters," she murmured. "I was that frightened for you. My love, my little love."

Norah didn't say anything. I got this sense of missing her, wishing for her to come back, to be holding my hand again.

"Where's Belle and Amy?" she asked when Bea let go of her.

I wanted to know that as well. I was scared for them all of a sudden. A relief to get Bea's answer, "They said they should come. Amy especially. I wouldn't let them. I took them to Mrs. Tocher's."

"They're safe then?" Norah let out.

"Safe as can be," Bea replied.

Safe as can be. I had another long stare up at where the fire had been. Safe as can be! How safe was that?

We'll have to go now, I thought to myself. Bea'll make us. I was wrong on that one. Seemed like she couldn't go from there any more than anyone else could, not once she'd come.

It was long after midnight before the crowd started thinning, before we all set into heading our separate ways. I don't think we even said goodbye to one another. I don't think we could trust ourselves to get the shape of any sort of farewell-speaking onto our lips.

All the way home, Bea was clutching at Norah's hand. Or maybe it was the other way around. I'm not certain. I just know I walked beside them, no one holding any longer onto me. First thing when we got to the building I wanted to see Belle and Amy. I wanted to touch them.

"No point in disturbing them," Bea announced.

Who was I to argue? She was their mother. Who was I to say I wanted it to be more than the three of us—going up the stairs, down the dark hallway, into the apartment, through the door?

March month, raw damp cold as ever. Wasn't till I was inside I noticed that same old tingling of cold-pain in my fingers and my toes. First time, too, I thought about how we hadn't had anything to eat. Bea was up to dealing with that problem. She had the soup we should have had for supper sitting in its pot. I suppose we drank it. I suppose there was some taste.

Next thing should've been bed. But it was so late. So much of the night gone already. Anyway, it came to me how most like Bea'd take Norah with her. They'd go to the bed in the bedroom together. I'd be on the pull-out by myself.

I didn't want that. It was better to be sitting with them, our chairs pulled up to the window. We weren't the only ones awake still.

"There's lights all over," Norah whispered.

There were too. Lights in all the buildings. All the families. Voices coming out of the air shaft from above and below. A great thick sadness hanging over everything, filling the air up. I didn't want to move hardly. Seemed like just me moving might shake the whole of the world.

I suppose I nodded off sometimes. I suppose we all did. Only thing I know really is it was getting light when the knock came on the door. Wasn't a tap this time either. There was a firmness to it, a determination.

Last person I expected to see on the doorstep when Bea opened up was Zeke. He wasn't pale any longer either. He was standing stiff. His cap was rammed on his head. His whistle was sticking out of his pocket like always.

He'd pulled himself into some hard kind of tightness. It was there in all of him. Like he was a soldier or some such.

"What are you here for?" Bea asked him.

"I'm doing my job. I'm selling papers." The words came as if he was spitting them out of him.

I tried to catch his eye but I couldn't.

"Not that I'll charge you," he added.

There was something in how he said it. A bitterness.

"What's up?" I demanded.

He looked directly at me.

"They've printed extra. Read all about it."

"Extra?"

"Don't you get it? I'm set to make more money today than I've made in one day ever."

So much hurting. He softened a bit. "I'm sorry," he said to us. "I know you probably don't even want a paper. I just needed to start with folks I know."

Then he was gone. With just the clatter of his boots to be hearing and Bea left in the doorway, holding the paper in her hands. She came back in. She set the paper on the table. As she did, it was like the headlines were shooting up at me.

Numbers again. Not like in the strike though. Numbers that were awful.

141 Men and Girls Die in Waist Factory Fire.

So there it was. How he was off to stand on some street corner, shouting the words like he had to.

Men and Girls Die.

Girls and men he'd talked to sometime maybe?

A hundred and forty-one. Yelling it over and over.

Men and Girls.

Girls who lived where he did? What did I know? Not just that anyway.

Street Strewn with Bodies.

Bodies he'd heard falling.

Selling, smiling. "Thank you, sir. Thank you, miss. Thank you, lady."

Selling, selling, selling.

Piles of Dead Inside.

What kind of place was it? I wondered. What kind of a place where someone who wasn't hardly more than a boy still, not even up to my shoulder. Someone, anyone had to do that?

Belle and Amy came not long afterwards. They might not have been there—at Triangle—but they knew sure enough something bad had happened. They were solemn, quiet, as they gave each of us a hug. There was no giggling and chattering from them as Bea made breakfast. They just did what they were supposed to—Belle setting out the cutlery, Amy reaching down the bowls.

The newspaper was on a shelf by that time. Bea had put it up there, right as they got in the apartment, hiding the pictures from them. It was Norah fetched the paper down once we'd eaten our oatmeal.

"Will you read it for me?" she asked me.

How could I say no to her? Wasn't it bad enough she couldn't read it for herself? Although why would she want to?

Why did I? I don't know. I don't know. Maybe it was the same as not covering my eyes, my ears. Norah hadn't done that either, had she?

"If that's what you're about, you're to go in the bedroom," Bea told us. "You're to do it by yourselves."

She started getting ready what was needed so Belle and Amy could help her with the buttons, although I could see her hands were shaking as she threaded a needle for herself. I'd thought maybe she'd have taken them to church. She did that sometimes. Sometime in St. John's I'd stopped going. I couldn't get the feel of it like I'd had in Atterley. Apparently church wasn't in Bea's plan.

Amy got this look on her face. "We should be able to know properly," she argued.

Gave me a bit of a shock. Made me think how old she was getting. She'd just had her birthday. She'd reached the age of ten. Norah had been at the pulling since she was nine now, hadn't she? She'd told me. There were younger ones than that even. I saw them every day.

I could tell Bea was unsure as to what to answer. After all, she knew what was coming on Amy's road. Maybe she'd been planning it even. A bit more money.

"You could be right," she said finally. "You could be, but you'll have to wait. You'll have to because I can't stand it at the moment and that's flat."

Her voice was strict enough to make Amy pick up her own needle, even if she didn't look too pleased about it.

Off we went—me and Norah—into the bedroom, closing the door behind us. Norah sat on the bed edge. I sat beside her, holding the paper so she could look over my shoulder though there wasn't much use to her doing it.

New York Times, March 26, 1911.

I got through that bit all right. I headed on into *Three stories of a ten-floor building at the corner of Greene Street and Washington Place were burned yesterday.*

I thought Norah might stop me any minute. She didn't.

She just put her hand on my knee. Once more, too, her grip kept tightening. Why wouldn't it?

The screams, the falling. Hearing about it from the writing... It was like we were standing there all over again.

There was stuff that was new to us. Dreadful stuff.

A heap of corpses lay on the sidewalk.

The first living victim, Hyman Meshel of 322 East Fifteenth was found paralyzed with fear and whimpering like a wounded animal in the basement.

Stuff that was just more details. Details to make everything worse.

Nothing human about most of those ... being taken in a steady stream to the Morgue.

Thirty bodies clogged the elevator shaft.

To identify them by a tooth or the remains of a burned shoe.

Thousands of people...were screaming with horror at what they saw.

Don't jump, don't jump, don't jump.

Took forever for me to get to the end of the front page even.

"That's not the whole of it, is it?" Norah said, when I did.

"There's more on page four," I had to tell her.

"Will you read that to me as well?" she asked me.

I turned the pages, the rustle of the turning seeming so loud. Pages four and five were stuck together. I had to wet my finger and work at the top corner to open them. Page four is where the names of the dead were listed.

Surely she won't want to hear those, I thought to myself. I was wrong though. She sat there, still as still.

ABERSTEIN, JULIA, 30 years.

ALTMAN, ANNA, 16, 33 Pike Street.

BERNSTEIN, MOSES, 800 East 5th Street.

BINEVITZ, ABRAHAM, 30, 474 Powell Street.

BIREMAN, GUSSIE, 22, 8 Rivington Street.

CAPUTTA, 17 years, 81 Degraw Street, Brooklyn.

CREPO, ROSE, 19 years, an Italian.

DENENT, FRANCES, 20 years.

DORMAN, K., (man,) identified by registered letter receipt, 235 Gold Street, Brooklyn.

FEICISCH, REBECCA, 17, Russian, 10 Attorney Street, Burns on body: St.Vincent's Hospital.

LAUNSWOLD, FANNIE, 24 years.

All so neat, in alphabetical order. Put there A to Z. There were those we knew too, each one of them bringing her own bit of grief to us. I couldn't go on. I just couldn't. I thought if I did any more I'd never want to hear my own voice speaking anything again. I stopped. I put the paper down.

"I'll finish it later."

Norah stood up. "Mum might want a cup of tea," she said to me.

I should've gone with her maybe—back into the kitchen— but somehow I didn't. Somehow I just stayed sitting there. Somehow the paper got itself into my hands again.

Unidentified Dead.

GIRL, 15 years: all clothing burned off except black stockings and black lace shoes.

ITALIAN WOMAN, 27 years, 5 feet 7 inches, red waist, black stockings, and skirt, no shoes, yellow metal ring on left hand set with blue stone.

WOMAN, 30 years, 5 feet 2 inches black hair, handbag containing $10.

WOMAN, 21 years, 5 feet: two rings, one with three small stones and another with three small white stones.

Thirty nine bodies burned beyond recognition.

Reported Missing.

Norah had closed the door behind her. Door or no door, I could hear Bea's voice reaching through to me. Letting Norah know if she actually wanted the kettle to boil she was going to have to put more wood in the stove. Telling Belle she should pick up something she'd dropped. Giving Amy a nudge to move the work along faster.

Wasn't Bea I wanted, all of a sudden. All of a sudden I had those words from so long ago in my head again. "Mum, oh Mum."

You're a great grown girl of eighteen, I told myself. You're a woman nearly.

Still I could see her. I could smell her almost—bread-making day when she was all yeasty and floury or when she'd come in from the garden, when she had the scent of the vegetables on her. Bigger than Bea, softer.

"Will you have some tea too?" Norah called out to me.

I drank what she'd made but there was still the rest of the paper to be got through with her. Long before I was done with it, I had the answer to my question—the one I'd asked myself when Zeke had gone from us. It was in my head. It was pounding, repeating itself over and over.

A terrible place. That's where we were living. Wasn't only the fire, now was it? There was a list of ills so long you'd never get through it.

A terrible place. Terrible. That's where we all were.

"Will we go to work tomorrow?" Norah asked, when we'd made it to the end of the day at last.

What had we done with ourselves in all those hours between? I wondered. Yes, there'd been neighbours come

calling. Mrs. Tocher and more beside her. Talk and talk
and talking. The dread of it. But what about the rest of the
time? I had no idea. I just knew that Sunday was over. It was
finished with.

"I can't imagine Global's going to close itself up. Hell'd
freeze over more likely," Bea answered.

I hate to say it but there was a relief in her almost. Norah
and me—we knew the reason. Of course we did. A day's pay!
There we were then—the two of us—the next morning, up
and ready, setting off together, same as always, except for
how—as we got nearer—Norah took hold of my hand once
more. I felt her trembling. She wasn't the only one that was
frightened. Truth is, I wasn't too steady myself. The newspaper
had said the fire had maybe started in a scrap bin. Scrap bins!
The sleeve room had scrap bins all over. More than our job's
worth to try to empty them. Who knew why? Another rule that
was simply there to plague us. Each one of those scrap bins full
to bursting, each one of them sitting there waiting for a spark
of something, I supposed.

And weren't we like ants in an ant hill? Even if the doors
weren't locked on us. All those rows and rows of us sitting
there. Weren't we crowded in like fish in a boat load? Weren't
we like those Triangle girls?

Up to the second-floor sleeve room we went anyway.
Angelika, Rebekkah, Rachele, Paolina, Reen—all of us coming
in, taking our coats off, getting ourselves ready. Quick sort
of hugs to give each other strength.

"Will you be all right?" I asked Norah.

She'd got her wish. She was at a machine, two rows in front
of me. At least I'd be able to see her.

"Of course I will," she said.

I hoped so. Oh, I hoped so.

I sat myself down. I waited for the power to come on. OK, I thought, OK.

Two minutes we got "for silence in acknowledgment of the regrettable incident that has taken place among us." Mr. Spengler's very words. No mention of how the whole thing might have been avoided. No mention of people being trapped. No mention of how there were those among us who'd got black armbands on them. Those whose faces were heavy with weeping. Those that actually had loved ones who'd been lost.

It was business as usual. Same old bundles. Same old sleeves arriving, same old pushing them under the needle. Same old thrum and thrum and thrumming of machines. Like nothing had happened. *Nothing*.

"Can you believe it?" I burst out when we got our lunch break.

Trouble was we all could easily enough.

Rebekkah unwrapped her bagel. She folded up the paper to be used again. "Momma says it feel like pogrom."

"And what's that, in the name of heaven?" I asked her.

I wished I'd been a bit more gentle when she turned her eyes down, when she sighed before she gave us the answer, folding and unfolding the paper again.

"When soldiers come, in the old country, on horses, with swords, with guns, burn homes, steal everything, kill people."

Rebekkah swallowed. Everyone was silent once more.

There's no soldiers in Atterley. That's what hit me, out of the blue, coming on me like a load of squid.

Same as when I'd thought of Mum too. As if I could see it. As if I was there. On a fine summer day. The men on the water still, not back with their catches yet. The women spreading the fish out for drying on the flakes. The sea just lapping. A little bit of a breeze blowing in the grasses.

Seemed so peaceful. Seemed so good.

Rebekkah was going on, "Momma say we have to be thankful no pogroms here. She say is same now. We don't stop. Like there, people hide. When they come out, they weep but still must keep on working."

"My papa, he say we have to be forgetting." That was Paolina.

Forget? I thought to myself. Some chance of that.

Some chance, for sure.

Straight after work, not saying we were going to do it even, we found ourselves walking along the streets to where the Triangle building was. Standing about outside the police cordon, seeing the broken top windows, the stains on the sidewalk that'd maybe never come out. Looking at that useless mangled fire escape hanging there.

I'd lay money we all of us had the screams and the falling there in us. Me, Angelika, Rebekkah, Paolina, Rachele, Reen with her cane.

Norah was back at my side. She was clutching my hand again. She was, then she wasn't. She was taking herself off. She was going to that cordon. She was lifting it, as if she was about to get under it so I had to be hurrying to grab her. When I did she struggled against me, trying to pull herself away.

"What d'you think you're doing?" I asked her.

She looked at me as if she hardly knew me. As if she had to bring herself out of some nightmare. She started crying.

"I could've been there."

"Of course you couldn't."

"Yes, yes, I could. I went. I asked for a job. It was one lunch time. I thought I'd never be taken on as an operator at Global.

I thought I'd always be a puller. They didn't have a place for me."

"At *Triangle?*"

"I would've gone there in an instant."

Norah. Not Norah!

She was crying harder. All I could do was hold her. Like Bea had done, only different. I was too shocked.

The others had heard. They came crowding. I wanted one of them to say something to her but no one did at first. It took each of them a while to get to some place where they could even touch her. They were good then. All of them had some word to offer her.

Reen was the best. She held onto both of us.

"Hard to bear. Hard to bear," she kept whispering. Like she was telling us whatever it was we were feeling, we had a right.

We were late home again, of course, the two of us. Norah wasn't going to go back till her tears had dried and her eyes weren't red any more.

"You'll not tell Mum, will you?" she demanded, as we reached the building.

Seemed like there was only one way to answer. "Not if you don't want me to."

"I don't. She's got enough. I don't want her worrying more."

That was it then. Hard to bear, hard to bear.

All through supper I found myself looking across the table at her, thinking how her chair might be empty. Worse too. I could see her falling. Her skirts all billowing around her, her braid come loose. I saw it in the evening and I saw it in my dreams.

I had to get up from the bed to bring myself out of it. There were lights all over that night too. Nightmares everywhere. Plain enough.

We did get a day off from Global for the Memorial Parade. Row upon row of us again, only now we were in clothes of mourning. A long, great river of blackness. Going where we'd gone in strike time. Just the sound of our feet, moving and moving over the pavement. Deep silence upon us, us and the watchers. Bands playing slow, sad music that'd break your heart.

Banners for the Unions to make clear we weren't stupid. We knew there'd been injustice. Banners not just for ILGWU, but for the Women's Trade Union League, for the American Federation of Labor even. Unity coming deeper out of sorrow, so it seemed. Rain that fell pouring, drenching. Some of the dead already buried. The others in coffins pulled by horses, with the families behind. Some of those coffins known to be so...so almost empty.

Me and Norah and Angelika and Rebekkah and Reen and Rachele and Paolina beside one another. Not linking arms, but in a line.

One hundred and forty-six!!! More even than Zeke's newspaper had said that first day after. So many that'd gone from us.

"My Adele."

"My Maria."

So many who were never coming back.

A terrible place. Terrible.

How could I not be thinking about Atterley? How could I not be wanting to there? Seeing her who meant so much to me. Mum, oh Mum.

I mean, I'd had bad times before. There'd been all the things I told about already. But now it was like they were piled up together. The off-season not-working, the being cold and hungry, little Sheena. The prodding—the prodding especially. Everyone else with difficulties that were just as bad. Worse, in fact, often. Much worse.

No homes for some, like Zeke had been that summer. Living in doorways. The families—the families that did have empty seats. Hard and hard, so it was as if there was some huge mountain, weighing upon us. Us in the tenements, the factories. No getting out of it. No way through.

When we were good people. Good. I'd seen it. I'd felt it, hadn't I, coming home that night there. I'd had it in my bones.

Even during the parade I was picturing them all—my family. Seeing them through my tears. They were standing at the door of the house to welcome me. Not just Mum and Dad, but Jim and Pete and Winnie and Tess and Will and Johnny and Harry and yes, yes, my little Janie, that I could take to hold again at last. I kept hearing them saying how much they'd missed me, how glad they were to have me back home.

After, in the days that followed, the seeing them went on coming. It got so bad I actually sat down and wrote a letter. In it I put how maybe it was Winnie's turn "to go on an adventure." Maybe she could be sending the money that was needed instead of me. I got to the end. I read it over. I was horrified at myself. How could I? How could I? I tore the whole thing up. I shoved the pieces in the stove and burned them. I can't say that was the end of it. I can't say I wasn't tempted into thinking I might set myself to write the very same words to Mum again.

And there was no escape. Everywhere was all a seething. There was a whole new slew of meetings to be attending. The Union leaders were saying the owners of Triangle should be "brought to justice." They should be made to pay

compensation to the families. The Union leaders wanted us
to know they were doing this fundraising. To help those that
had been made so they couldn't work any longer, those that
were dependent on those that had been killed.

Shouting and shouting.

Nothing was the same as it had been either. Nothing
and no one. I could see how Norah was having trouble getting
herself through the Global sleeve-room door each day.
I could hear how…We'd sing a bit—the girls. There wasn't
the same energy to it though. There was a lot of crying over
God knows what that usually didn't matter—needles that
got broken, bundles that weren't picked up quick enough.
Angelika started weeping one day because she'd left her lunch
at home, for heaven's sake! Angelika who always laughed
at herself.

I knew, sure enough, I was needed. I knew most like it was
my rent money that was keeping Amy from the pulling table.
I knew about the others that had been renters before me that
had been trouble.

And Norah…there was more than once I had to put my
arms around her in the nighttime. More than once I woke
to her shaking me, "Edie, Edie please."

Zeke too. He kept showing up where I was, wanting to play
me a tune or something. Getting me to talk to him about the
day we'd had together, getting me to remind him how he'd
made those children happy. Looking for some company he
couldn't get out of anyone else.

In the sleeve room as well… Angelika and Rebekkah, Reen
and Rachele, Paolina. We were more than friends by that time.
If one of us was down, the others'd do something—anything—
to help out.

I did know I was needed. Didn't stop me sneaking off to the docks now and then to check on what boats might be going. Didn't stop me thinking what I might do to get together the money for the fare.

That's not the whole of it even. I began having this notion that had to do with Mum. I imagined how... Say if she broke her leg. The work'd be too much for Winnie. I'd have to go, wouldn't I? I'd have to be there to do what had to be done.

I thought about it so much I sort of convinced myself it was going to happen. Must have been that, mustn't it? Must have been why I was so particularly excited when I came in from work to find an envelope with the address in Mum's writing propped up on the kitchen table where letters for me always went.

We'd got into kind of a thing with all she sent me. Bea had asked me about it one time, way, way back. I'd read out to her what was on the pages. She'd asked me again the next time. It'd come to be a habit. There was never anything specially private. Just Mum letting me in on what everyone was doing—how Jim had a girl friend from across the bay and Tess was growing faster than anyone could keep up with dressing her. Stuff like that.

Bea liked hearing it because it was about the Island.

"Takes me back," she said to me.

Mum had a nice way of writing too. In the beginning there'd just been Bea who listened, but Norah and Belle and Amy had got drawn in as well. They'd gather around. None of them ever seemed to get tired of any of it. They seemed to be always hoping for more. That's why I didn't open the letters till after supper, after we'd eaten and everything was cleared away.

As I ate I did worry a bit, considering how I was so certain what was going to be inside. I thought maybe I should try saying I had a headache or some such. I wasn't up to the out-loud business.

Came to me though, as the meal went on. Perhaps having the news delivered that way might be perfect, better in fact than if I had to be announcing it myself. I mean, everyone'd be able to see how surprised I was. How sorry to be leaving them in the lurch.

Supper got done fast. It always did on letter days. Bea made tea. We sat at the table. I was a little nervous as I put my thumb under the flap to tear the envelope open but not too much. I took the letter out. I unfolded it.

The words were all a scrawl. I'd never seen anything like it.

"Don't be keeping us waiting," Bea said.

I gulped. There wasn't even a *Dear Edie*.

"I'm that riled. I've had it up to here with the lot of them. It's washday Monday. The line's broken and the sheets are trailing in the mud. The rain's pouring down. I'm going to have to start over. The house is like a dust heap. I went outside to the well to get more water. While I was at it your precious Janie and Harry got themselves in a tussle. They started throwing flour at one another from the bin. It's flour I need for baking. Your father's been working in the garden, supposedly getting it ready for planting. Tramping in mud all over more like seems to me. Jim and Pete have been with him. I don't know what's got into them. Why can't they remember to take their boots off? What's with this, "I'll only be a minute?" If I could get my hands on them right now, I'd wring their necks. What would be the use of that? you ask. I suppose you'd be right but here we are,

another season coming. I find myself dreading it. All that fish
to be carrying, spreading, turning. No rest for the wicked
as the saying goes so I guess the wicked must be me. Could
anything else go wrong? Well, yes, it could. The rain's turned
to sleet. Winnie went off to school without getting the wood
in like it's her day to be doing. The stove needs stoking for me
to be heating the soup for lunch. I've nothing to put in it.
The stove, I mean. Not a single log. Also I got in a fight with
Liz's mother. I told her I was sick to death of her going on
and on about how Liz is becoming quite the lady with this latest
boyfriend she's got herself. 'Tell me another,' I said to her.
She didn't like that at all. She went all haughty on me. If you
want the truth I think your friend, Liz, is no better than she
should be. No doubt you'll catch my meaning. I suppose you
might call this ranting. I suppose you'd be right in that as well.
All I can say is I've written you a lot of nice letters and this
isn't one of them."

That was it. No love. Not her name even, just her initials.
M. M. (nee N).

Margaret Murphy that was Neal.

Mum, oh Mum!

I did my best to keep from laughing but my shoulders
were shaking. I could feel the chuckles bubbling in my throat.
It's not I wasn't sorry for her. I'd seen her on days like that.
I knew she was beside herself. I knew she felt like she was
being tortured.

The way she'd written it though, in such a scramble.
It was kind of funny. And anyway there was my "paradise"
in all its glory. My paradise in all its lovely, peaceful goodness.
Every living moment of it.

"The world of the worker," Bea said.

All I could think was how I must have been off my head.

The women quiet at the flakes! How had I come up with that one? Flake work was brutal. Hadn't I felt that? Hadn't I had it in all of my body when I was there?

Bea wasn't even trying to restrain herself. She was chortling with abandon.

"I'll have none of that nonsense with the flour from you," she told Belle and Amy, wagging her finger at them.

They shrank down like they were frightened but it was only pretend.

"Nonsense with the flour." Sounded like Janie might be something of a terror. Not quite the angel I'd been imagining. I remembered I'd had some hints of that in other things Mum had sent me. I just hadn't wanted to believe it.

"Could you read the letter again?" Norah asked, her eyes alight and dancing.

I hemmed and hawed a while, getting myself ready like it was a performance. I started a whole lot faster so it all seemed even more of a drama. Amy got into pounding on the table whenever I paused for breath. Norah made it like she was the piano player at one of those movies at the nickelodeon I talked about, building the suspense up.

I had to stop reading quite often. We were all of us laughing so much.

"Better bring your mum here so she can have a holiday," Bea joked, when I got to the end.

By then, we'd got tears of laughter running down our faces. We were filling the apartment with the sound.

"Next time you write to her, tell her I sympathize," Bea said, giving me and Norah and Belle and Amy a look that said we were the cause of all her woes.

When we'd finally pulled ourselves together, she got up.
She put the kettle on again. Belle cuddled up to me. She gave
me a kiss. The other two went into the living room to get on
with some button work before bedtime. All of sudden, I was
overcome with how much each one of them meant to me.
How simple and ordinary everything seemed.

Occurred to me I hadn't even told Mum about the
fire at Triangle. I hadn't wanted her being bothered.
There was none of them in Atterley knew anything about it,
far as I knew. Wasn't only the fire either, was it? There was
a whack of this, that, and the other I'd not written about.
I'd made my own "nice letters."

Gave me more than a few ideas to chew on, that did.
Same as always, I kept myself awake to do it. I lay in the
darkness beside Norah, working those ideas through.

A terrible place? A terrible place?

I *had* listened to the screams. I *had* seen and heard the
falling. I hadn't forgotten and I wasn't going to. I didn't even
believe forgetting was what had to be done. Remembering
was more like. Remembering, and not being beat.

But we weren't beat, were we? Look how it had been that
evening. How we'd enjoyed ourselves. How we'd had such fun.

Didn't that prove it? Didn't it? Didn't it?

Anyway, anyway…

How could I have thought I could up and leave and not miss
everyone? How could I have imagined that?

The fire wasn't everything. It wasn't.

And I wasn't the same old Edie. Not like I'd been when
I'd come.

I'd made a place for myself. I belonged there. It was true
there were folks I was needed by. Didn't I need them as well?

The next morning when I got out of bed and went off
to work I put a swing in my step. It wasn't I was making
the Island mean nothing to me. I couldn't. It wasn't possible.
Still I'd stopped being torn up with longing for it like I had
been that last while.

Strange how things happen. Not long after I got myself
a fellow. Giorgio, his name was. Everybody liked him. He was
kind and he was friendly. He took Zeke under his wing even.
God knows Zeke needed it. He needed a man to be on his side.

Did I ever go back to Atterley? Yes, yes, I did. Once I'd got
over finding Mum's letter funny, I'd been worried. I'd written
to her about how she should take care of herself. How I was
sorry she had so much on her plate. She'd written back to tell
me how she'd just been on a tear. In the end she'd had a bit
of a laugh herself.

I thought all was well but then I heard from Dad she'd
sprained her wrist. Winnie had gone off to St. John's by that
time. It was summer. Not much work in the sleeve room
anyway. Bea told me she'd manage. Come hell or high water
she wouldn't take in anyone else.

Big thing I did, once I'd been there a week or so and could
see how the land lay, was to sit everyone down. I gave them
a good talking to—Dad even. I told them they'd have to stop
taking Mum for granted. They weren't too pleased, any of
them. I could see they weren't really ready for a different me.

Mum was grateful I'd come. We had good times together.
Still, she seemed glad enough when I told her I couldn't
stay forever. Glad to know she was getting her own little
kingdom back.

The last night before I left there were stars again shining
in the darkness, there was wind in plenty to rattle the house

and whip up the sea. I took Janie's hand. I went outside with
her. She wasn't a terror. Not really. She just had a touch too
much in the way of energy. It was like the gales that had
rescued her had got inside her, like they were always trying
to make sure they weren't ignored.

"It was a night such as this when you were born," I said
to her, but I didn't go any further.

I kept the mystery of just how it had been to myself.

The fact was she believed she was like the rest of us.
She was Mum and Dad's own child. It was what Mum and Dad
had chosen to tell her because they reckoned it would be the
best for her. It was the way such things were dealt with.
Who was I to go messing with that?

Janie gave a little giggle. "Mum said about it," she told me.

We stood on together, feeling the fierceness that was all
around us. When I saw how she was tossing her head to catch
the wind in her hair more fully, it seemed to me the mystery
I'd known back then was in her. She understood about it.

"You'll do all right, you will," I said.

She went running inside, laughing louder. I stood on
by myself.

Months later Zeke put another newspaper in my hand. This one
had a headline said *Nobody Guilty*. The headline was followed
by a whole lot of writing that described how the Triangle
owners had got themselves some clever lawyer. Somehow
or other this lawyer had managed to prove that they themselves
(the owners) had not known about the door locking. They
themselves (the owners) had not been aware of the danger
of the scrap bins. They themselves (the owners) were not
responsible. They themselves (the owners) could not be held

to account. They themselves (the owners) were to be considered generous because they'd paid all the families the princely sum of $75 to make up for their loss!

Talk about being riled. Talk about wanting to wring some necks. All those that were dead and gone forever. Screaming, falling. Bodies twisted, bodies burned.

We marched against it. All of us from the sleeve room, all of us from Global, all of us from the Union it seemed. We knew we couldn't change the verdict. Didn't mean we didn't know there'd been a wrong. Didn't mean we weren't angry. Didn't mean our anger shouldn't be seen.

Going back to Atterley had made another difference to me. Felt like I'd got the wind and stars back in my feet and in my lungs. Seemed to me like I could hear the same thing in the feet and the voices of us all. When the march was done, the others went off to get themselves a soda. There was this new shop just opened. I didn't go with them. I didn't want to. What I wanted was to go to Triangle. That's what I did then. I went there again and I looked up. The floors that had been burned were all rebuilt by that time. Same conditions for the workers though, I'd heard plenty about that.

I shook my head. I made myself a promise. I promised I'd keep marching for all the life I had to live. I'd march till I couldn't march any longer. I'd march my feet off. I'd do whatever I could so we could keep pulling ourselves up by our boot straps, so we could make it so we mattered, so we had to be taken into account. We could have those changes that never should—not ever—have been things we had to fight for, things that never should—not ever—have been made to seem like they were only for our dreams.

Stars and stars and stars.

They weren't much of a feature in the night sky on the
Lower East Side I can tell you. It was all a haze. There was too
much crowding, too much smoke and stuff floating about in the
air. Still I knew if I waited till darkness and I looked carefully
I could see them. Some of them anyway. I could and I would,
always and ever, all through my days.

Photo: Chris Hibbs

POSTSCRIPT

Jan died on Sept. 2, 2017. After working on this book for more than 20 years, she will never see it. Over all that time, she went on believing in Edie, until finally her story began to take a shape that felt like a book. When she died, all but the smallest edits had been finished and *To See the Stars* was ready to go out into the world.

Jan grew up in England and that mattered to her. She knew the south downs were her natural landscape. But after immigrating to Canada as a young woman she grew to love this country passionately, especially perhaps its mountains and rivers. But there was something very particular in Newfoundland that held her, touched her deeply. She never lived there but visited often, and three of her four "chapter" books are set there.

Perhaps this was because she felt there was some deep kinship between the place and the people of Newfoundland and the place and the people she had left behind in England. Newfoundland is, like England, sea-girt and Jan loved the sea. But most of all I think it was a sense that many Newfoundlanders took on life with the kind of vitality that her family had always insisted on.

One of my favourite photos of Jan was taken in Cupids at a storytelling concert celebrating the town's 400th anniversary. In the photo she's telling "Cap o' Rushes," a classic English folk tale. In her introduction she talked about how her grandmother had been in service, like the old tale's heroine, like Edie. She reminded her audience about the everyday heroism of all those unheralded Newfoundlanders who have just gotten on with doing whatever work had to be done to survive. Some of Jan's earliest memories were of laughter and silliness in the face of bombs falling and then the drudgery of rationing after the war. In Newfoundland she found that same courage; the dancing, the music, the stories no matter what.

Always and always Jan knew, life is never easy. She knew this from the old tales she loved so much, from her keen observation of the world she lived in, from her families' history, from her own life. All her books, and this one is no exception, are about the fierce beauty of being alive even in the face of how hard that is. They're about how if we will dig deep enough, each and every one of us, just like Edie, can find inside what we need to live a good life, a life that insists on the possibility of joy.

~ Jennifer Cayley

ACKNOWLEDGEMENTS

I begin with an apology to all the people and organizations that supported
Jan in creating this book but who are not acknowledged here. I fear that
there are names I haven't found in my hunt through Jan's files: people she met
with and talked to who made a significant impact on this work, especially
as she researched the Newfoundland sections. If she hadn't died so suddenly
Jan would have gotten all those names out of her head and heart, and made
a complete list. So on Jan's behalf, I would thank all the people and
organizations listed below and also everyone who isn't named.

I do know she would want to acknowledge Marnie Parsons of Running
the Goat right up front. Marnie loved the book from the beginning. After
Jan's death, many publishers would have been tempted to drop the project.
Marnie never wavered and I can't tell you how much it has meant to me and
the rest of Jan's family that all those years of work are not wasted. Jan's agent
Marie Campbell has been similarly stalwart, listening, remembering,
always reminding me and everyone else about how good Jan's writing was.
Tara Bryan is also to be commended for looking deep into the book and into
the history to make just the right pictures to help lift the words off the page.

Jan would, I think, want to acknowledge my contribution because I did step
in and take on some final editing. As I worked, I was pretty sure Jan would
have been horrified if she'd known I was editing her words! But … being
the practical person she was, she would have recognized the necessity for this
and been grateful.

When she went to New York, Jan was deeply moved by her time in the
East Side Tenement Museum, which made it possible for her to see and feel
the fabric of Edie's life in New York. She was also very grateful for advice
from Eileen Kennedy Morales of the Museum of the City of New York.
The sections that Edie reads from the newspaper following the Triangle
Shirtwaist Factory Fire are quoted from the *New York Times*, March 26, 1911
edition. More than 100 years later, it is still heartbreaking to read this
contemporary account.

Patricia Fulton from Memorial University of Newfoundland and Labrador's
Folklore and Language Archives gave invaluable assistance with issues relating
to Newfoundland's social history. Scholar, singer, teller of tales, Anita Best

offered Jan important creative inspiration. Conversations with Anita helped Jan make a clear picture of Atterley, where Edie first sees the stars. Carmelita McGrath's keen ear for cadence and figures of speech helped Jan find Edie's voice and ensure that it had some real sense of the music and vividness of Newfoundland speech.

Last but certainly not least, thanks go to that splendid cultural institution, the Canada Council for the Arts, which gave Jan a major grant that allowed her a significant stretch of time to do almost nothing else besides live in and create the very particular world of *To See the Stars*.

~ Jennifer Cayley

This book was designed by Veselina Tomova of Vis-à-vis Graphics, St. John's,
Newfoundland and Labrador, and was printed in Canada.

978-1-927917176

Running the Goat, Books & Broadsides is grateful
to Newfoundland and Labrador's Department of Tourism, Culture, Industry
and Innovation for support of its publishing activities through the province's
Publishers Assistance Program.
We also acknowledge the support of the Canada Council for the Arts,
which last year invested $153 million to bring the arts to Canadians
throughout the country.
Nous remercions le Conseil des arts du Canada de son soutien.
L'an dernier, le Conseil a investi 153 millions de dollars pour mettre de l'art
dans la vie des Canadiennes et des Canadiens de tout le pays.

Newfoundland
Labrador

Canada Council   Conseil des arts
for the Arts   du Canada

Running the Goat
Books & Broadsides Inc.
General Delivery/54 Cove Road
Tors Cove, Newfoundland and Labrador A0A 4A0
www.runningthegoat.com